Rebel Mountain

Der Berg der Rebellen

Rebel Mountain

By

Kurt Eggers

Translated by Theodor Runen

ANTELOPE HILL PUBLISHING

English Translation Copyright © 2022 Antelope Hill Publishing

First printing 2022

Originally published in German as *Der Berg der Rebellen*, by Schwarzhäupter-Verlag, 1937.

English translation and annotations by Theodor Runen (treuerunen@gmail.com), 2022.

Cover art by Swifty.
Edited by Tom Simpson.
Formatted by Taylor Young.

Antelope Hill Publishing
www.antelopehillpublishing.com

Paperback ISBN-13: 978-1-956887-18-1
EPUB ISBN-13: 978-1-956887-19-8

Meiner Kameradin,
Traute

To my dear comrade,
Traute

The will, desires, and deeds of German men described within this book are founded in historical truth. Only the Black Guard Freikorps as well as the characters of Lieutenant Maßmann and his friends are elements of literary fiction.

Contents

Translator's Foreword xi

The Fever Pitch xv

Preface xvii

Rebel Mountain 1

The Aftermath: A Military and Political Appendix 177

Translator's Foreword

On November 11th, 1918, a delegation of the faltering German Empire gathered in a train car near Compiègne, to sign the armistice that would end World War I. Two days earlier, the November Revolution had forced the German emperor to abdicate, leading to the declaration of a new German Republic on the very same day. Taken in concert, these events ushered in what would later become known as the Weimar Republic, a highly ambivalent period in German history. Commonly glorified as the first real German democracy, the Weimar Republic was in fact a highly unstable state. Built in the wake of a mutiny-turned-revolution, it would experience a series of attempted coups and uprisings from both left- and right-wing groups, such as the Munich Soviet Republic, the Kapp Putsch, and the Ruhr uprising, all of which took place over a period of a mere twelve months in 1919 and 1920. Plagued by repeated bouts of political violence, hyperinflation and unemployment, the republic increasingly fragmented along political, economic and also paramilitary lines. One of these fragments is widely known as the Freikorps movement.

Originating in the mid-eighteenth century, the term Freikorps originally referred to a paramilitary unit made up of a broad mixture of both domestic and foreign volunteers, but also deserters and convicts. Freikorps were primarily deployed to bolster regular troops and disrupt enemy movements via guerrilla attacks on supply lines. After the end of World War I, Freikorps made a brief return due to stipulations in the Treaty of Versailles, limiting the German Reichswehr to a strength of one hundred thousand men, a mere fraction of the eleven million soldiers the German military had employed at the end of the war. While a large percentage of these men returned to civilian life, a significant number of former soldiers were absorbed by paramilitary units, such as the Freikorps. Together with cadets, students and other volunteers, these veterans turned their attention to combating domestic threats, typically in the form of communist or socialist uprisings. Yet the Freikorps themselves were by no means enthusiastic supporters of the new republican government, as can be seen by their involvement in right wing coups like the Kapp Putsch or the famous 1923 Beer Hall Putsch by Adolf Hitler and the NSDAP. When Freikorps did support the Weimar government, it was typically out of a concern for the public order, based on a notion of choosing the lesser of two evils, with the status quo republican government generally seen as preferable to communist rule.

This was the world Kurt Eggers grew up in. Born in 1905, he was a mere thirteen years old when he took part in quelling the 1919 Spartacist uprising, an amalgamation of a general strike and various armed clashes in Berlin. Approximately one year later, he joined the short-lived Kapp Putsch against the Weimar government. Yet another year later, at fifteen years old, he would be closely involved in the Freikorps defense of Upper Silesia against Polish insurgents which provides the historical backdrop for *Rebel Mountain*.

While this book is primarily a work of fiction, it should be noted that Eggers personally participated in the famous reconquest of Annaberg, a small mountain which had previously been occupied by Polish troops. Eggers joined the battle as a member of the Black Band Freikorps, led by one lieutenant Bergerhoff, who also appears as a character in the later segments of this book. This is not the only autobiographic detail Eggers inserted into Rebel Mountain—throughout the narrative we can find evidence of his personal life and interests, in the names of certain rightwing and anti-Semitic associations, enthusiastic references to Ulrich von Hutten (a recurring role model in Eggers' works) or the curious appearance of a young recruit under the age of sixteen who happens to share the author's initials. And although we can assume Eggers to have been involved in some violent scenarios during the Spartacist uprising and the Kapp Putsch, Annaberg would likely have been his first real battle, making *Rebel Mountain* a deeply personal book for him.

But *Rebel Mountain* is more than a mere fictionalized recollection of autobiographic events. Published in 1937, it looks at the Freikorps phenomenon from a uniquely National Socialist and folkish perspective, while also reflecting on Eggers' prominent warrior philosophy. Whereas other Freikorps authors such as Ernst von Salomon focus on a kind of martial adventurer's spirit as the main motivation behind their fighting on the eastern border, the characters in *Rebel Mountain* display complex social and ultimately ethno-racial dynamics. Rather than showcasing individualized fighters eager for adventure and glory, Eggers portrays his fighters in the context of family and tribal relations. And although the Upper Silesian coal mines and factories are being considered as important economic factors, the main motivation of Eggers' rebels clearly lies in protecting the local German population from hardship and violence at the hand of Polish insurgents.

In portraying this fight against overwhelming odds, Eggers goes beyond mere patriotism. His rebels are not defending a state or a social order. Their fight reaches deep into the German ideal of an underlying *Volksgemeinschaft*, a racial union going beyond established concepts like monarchism, political parties and even the Church, particularly in its Catholic and Ultramontane denominations. *Rebel Mountain* is the story of an adventure, a departure from an ever-more suffocating society, toward the roots of a great people and its ever-so-elusive dreams of freedom.

The efforts of the Freikorps would ultimately be overturned by a hostile political establishment. Yet they persist as a powerful illustration of the tremendous impact that even a small group of dedicated men can have on world affairs.

Theodor Runen
February 12th, 2022

The Fever Pitch

November 9th, 1918	Death of Germany's honor.
November 18th, 1918	Without a declaration of war, Polish units occupy border towns in Posen.
December 15th, 1918	Cutting of diplomatic ties between Germany and Poland.
Early 1919	Weak German border troops are forced to retreat by Polish forces.
February 6th, 1919	Preliminary ceasefire between Germany and Poland.
May 7th, 1919	Dictate of Versailles.
June 28th, 1919	German traitors sign the Dictate of Versailles.
August 17th–24th, 1919	First Polish uprising in Upper Silesia.
August 19th–25th, 1919	Second Polish uprising in Upper Silesia
March 20th, 1921	Referendum in Upper Silesia: 707,000 votes for Germany, 479,000 votes for Poland.
May 3rd, 1921	Third Polish uprising in Upper Silesia.
May 21st, 1921	Annaberg is taken by German Freikorps. Germany's honor is resurrected.

Preface

History is born from deed!

Deeds, in turn, are born from ideas and desires, from recognitions and demands.

Will is not always driven by knowledge, often it is hardship that matures men into warriors.

Yet wherever a warrior rises, the shadows of hardship and disgrace succumb to the victorious light of his will.

A sharp sword is the ultimate comfort, the ultimate freedom. Happy the man who knows how to wield it in times of great change: amidst fall and decline, doubt and despair, he carries a message. By virtue of their deeds, the strong push open the gate to freedom and rule.

Blessed is the man whose heart grows firm: in risking grand leaps, in stumbling, he gains safe ground.

I shall tell of the leap from stumbling, of the leap risked by German men, when Germany was still shrouded in darkness. I shall write of their soul, which slowly rose from fearful paralysis and finally attained the ultimate freedom, as their lonely hearts prepared themselves to make the ultimate sacrifice. The Freikorps were waging a war for Annaberg, the holy mountain of Germany. A humble objective, measured against the seas of blood spilt during the Great War. Yet it appears colossal and worthy of worship when measured by the spirit of these men, who voluntarily went out to chase an almost hopeless destiny, to follow the decree of their blood, urging them to follow the laws of honor and duty.

The secret nation crowned them as heroes, those men who lost their home and were called enemies to the state.

By virtue of their battles and suffering, they cleared our people's flag, sullied by treason and guilt.

Honor to their deed, for it is history!

Honor to their desire! Amidst weary and worthless times, it led them to find the sword of the warrior.

As long as a people
Still brings forth warriors,
It is just!

Rebel Mountain

The Year 1921

"This was not the faith to move mountains—this was the faith to storm them."

Chapter 1

"Constable Riehl, you're headed to Herderstraße with three men. You know the place: the little bakery. And be careful!" The constable rises from his footstool and stands to attention. "Yes, Lieutenant!"

While the four policemen are slowly getting ready, awkwardly checking their pistols and adjusting their shakos, a young, gaunt constable has risen from his seat and is now headed for the door.

"Where to, Lemke?"

"Just dropping off a letter, sir."

The lieutenant eyes him with suspicion as the man hurries away. *Obscure fellow, this Lemke guy! Thinks too much, reads books, goes to meetings! Friendly with former Baltic fighters!*[1] The lieutenant is getting angry. Lemke better not cause him any trouble. There is already more than enough trouble in these crazy times. Break-ins, strikes, revolts: that's plenty for his service. No more! Anything but those damned politics. A rotten business, fit for suicidal maniacs. Ideals! Well and good for confirmands and volunteers. But don't you dare bother someone who volunteered for the war and had to live through November 1918 with your ideals!

The lieutenant pauses. *Lemke was on his way to the mailbox, wasn't he? So why is he going for the telephone booth?*

Constable Lemke feeds the coin into its slot, asking for Steinplatz 4518. *Jesus Christ, it takes way too long to get an answer.* Finally!

---

[1] Shortly after the end of the First World War in late 1918, German Freikorps were formed to halt the Soviet advances into Latvia and Lithuania, thereby preserving important buffer zones for East Prussia. The Baltic campaigns saw severe disagreements and open disobedience on the part of the Freikorps against the Weimar government, ultimately leading to an end of the Baltic campaigns in late 1919.

"Steinplatz 4518."
"Heenemann Bakery?"
"Yes, sir."
"Please call Mr. Maßmann."

Lemke is getting impatient. Every additional minute is suspicious, because the mailbox is only a few yards away from the Zoologischer Garten police station.

"Karl?"
"Yes?"
"You'll be getting some visitors. Four men. In about fifteen minutes."
"Thank you, got it."
"Over and out!"
"Over and out!"

Lemke slams down the receiver, satisfied.

At the police station, he bumps into commando Riehl.

"Good luck, Riehl."

Riehl, a die-hard Social Democrat, gives him a good-natured smile. "We'll get those bastards eventually, Lemke, and that will be it for those never-ending adventures of theirs."

Lemke's features are hardening as he looks after the four policemen headed to Hardenbergstraße.

Devil knows, playing hide-and-seek with comrades is not a pretty sight. But the men on Herderstraße are closer to this soldier's heart. And now they are warned.

A hand rests heavily on Lemke's shoulder.

The lieutenant!

"When did you start sending your letters via phone booth, Lemke?"

"Just a little white lie, Lieutenant. I had to call my girl!"

The lieutenant scrutinizes the constable from narrow eyes.

"You aren't being particularly careful."

Lemke pulls himself together and looks at his superior officer with clear eyes.

"Perhaps there exists a higher loyalty in this world. One which excuses even great imprudences."

The lieutenant is not comfortable with this kind of talk; by no means did he want to start a political discussion. He simply wanted to give the constable some advice, just between colleagues. After all, Lemke had once been a brave non-commissioned officer, who had faced off the enemy and received both the Silver Wound Badge and the Iron Cross First Class.[2]

"You have to come to your senses, Lemke. The war is over. You've risked your head more than enough times. And you have sworn an oath to uphold the Republic."

Lemke's face has taken on a contemptuous air.

"Unfortunately this rather excessive turnover of oaths has resulted in a devaluation."

The lieutenant's voice turns quiet.

"I did not hear that. This would be reason enough for a treason trial."

Lemke remains quiet, but his face still displays sneering contempt.

The lieutenant has become nervous. He resents having to admit that he is offended by his subordinate's superior spirit.

"I will be watching you. Behave yourself accordingly."

"Yes, sir!"

Lemke checks the time. Five minutes until his next patrol.

It is a cold winter. There hasn't been such hard frost in living memory. Freezing northeastern winds cut against human skin.

Constable Riehl curses under his breath. Berlin is a damned madhouse. Nothing but criminals and revolutionaries here. Both right- and left-wing. What on earth made him think putting in for a transfer from Opole[3] to Berlin was a good idea?

He had always been a good Social Democrat, no doubt about that. For ten years now he has been paying his party dues. Secretly at first, publicly boasting later. That should entitle him to a position in higher service after all. But Berlin is a disappointment. Where is the city's famed cheerfulness?

---

[2] The Wound Badge was a military decoration similar to the American Purple Heart, first established in 1918, the final year of World War I. The Wound Badge came in three classes, Black (wounded once or twice), Silver (wounded three or four times) and Gold (wounded five or more times).
The Iron Cross was a decoration primarily awarded to military men, but also some non-combatants. The Iron Cross First Class was much harder to acquire than the Second Class version, with only 218,000 Iron Crosses First Class being awarded during World War I, as opposed to approximately 5,200,000 Iron Crosses Second Class.
[3] Opole is a city located in modern-day Poland and the historical capital of Upper Silesia. A part of Prussia since the mid-eighteenth century, the city became a part of Poland after the end of World War II, its political assimilation accompanied by an expulsion of ethnic Germans. Approximately two-to-five percent of modern-day Opole residents are ethnic Germans, as opposed to approximately ninety-four percent of residents with German nationality in 1858.

These are starved people, without vitality or warmth.

And girls? They have those in Opole as well.

Constable Riehl starts a conversation about the folkish movement.[4] Whoever might be funding them? Do his companions think they are already preparing for the next war?

The other three are taciturn. What do they care about the folkish?! They're here to do their job, and that's that!

There are only a few people out on the streets. A sausage-dealer selling his wares. Constable Riehl shudders when he considers the contents of these suspicious-smelling sausages. Just recently, a killer was arrested, who processed his exclusively female victims into such sausages. The exact same kind that were sold in the streets of Berlin, typically around midnight.

What a horrible city! Such a thing would have been unthinkable in Opole.

A couple of whores try to get the policemen's attention, their shrill voices clamoring for victims.

But today, not even a drunkard would consider helping himself to those pathetic creatures, blue and frozen as they are.

Not even their uniforms are safe from the solicitations of these female individuals in their short and saucy skirts.

Constable Riehl casts a reprimanding glance at the youngest of his comrades, who exchanged a few crude jokes with one of these painted women.

They can already see the first few houses of Herderstraße. Everything wrapped in peaceful darkness.

Who would still have lights on at this hour anyway? Your average citizen is so frightened that he crawls into bed at ten o'clock in the evening and begs his dear God to let him awake the next morning without getting plundered—if it's not too much to ask.

They have reached Heenemann's bakery, harmless and sleepy.

The four policemen stop for a moment. In the house opposite the bakery, a lamp flares up for just a second.

Constable Riehl laughs disdainfully.

He knows that this is Louise Ostade's place, that little Flemish girl, the

---

[4] The folkish movement (*Völkische Bewegung*) was a racial movement that originated in the late nineteenth century, focused on bringing about a society based on German racial principles. Prominent characteristics of the movement included its pagan, traditionalist, and anti-Semitic currents. Despite the pagan image often associated with it, in reality the folkish movement was a broad, heterogeneous association of different religous currents, resulting in a relative coexistence of pagan and Christian groups.

bride of Lieutenant Maßmann. She followed her sweetheart from Belgium.

Constable Riehl is very familiar with the lives of these adventurers, those obstinate insurgents and front soldiers, who have chosen the Heenemann's bakery as a cauldron for their crazy ideas and plans! But the girl's warning won't save them this time! It takes him just a few leaps to reach the gate from which Louise is about to slip out.

"Hold it! Keep it together, missy!"

Louise lets out a shrill scream.

Riehl gets rough.

"Shut it, you stupid brat!"

Louise allows herself a quiet smile. Karl has been warned.

She is almost a little disappointed when Riehl returns a few minutes later. Snorting with rage, he has to admit that there is nothing suspicious to be found at Heenemann's bakery.

There they are, sitting harmlessly around the table in Heenemann's cozy living room: Lieutenant Karl Maßmann, working as a newspaper advertiser for the Berliner Lokal-Anzeiger, Sergeant Paul König, called "Napoleon," an epithet he earned because of his constant strategic objections in the Baltics, Sergeant Felix Teuscher, who sells parachutes and insurance policies with König, Private Xaverl Fuchsberger, who originally just wanted to come to Berlin to visit his lieutenant Maßmann but got stuck and turned into a stand-in for selling the eight o'clock evening paper, supposedly to meet more people.

Then there is the 1917 war volunteer Martin Harke who has reinvented himself as a student of philosophy. And although Harke is the funniest and cheekiest of them all, Baker Heenemann isn't too far off when it comes to independence of spirit and juiciness of idioms. Mrs. Heenemann (Harke calls her Marjelly), a nice, young, carefree girl from East Prussia, seems to be in a good mood.

"Won't you at least take a seat, Officer? We were having so much fun with the game. Don't get angry!"[5]

A nervous Riehl drums his thick fingers against the table, causing the soul-destroying game's tokens to dance around the board.

The policemen grin sheepishly. There is always something shameful about an unsuccessful raid. They couldn't even find the tiniest of pistols.

---

[5] Don't get angry! (*Mensch ärgere dich nicht!*) is a popular German board game invented in the early twentieth century and introduced to a larger audience in 1914. Its main objective is to reach a target area without getting sent back to the start by other players (and not getting too angry in the process).

Harke gets up, his long legs stalking toward the old piano, a cheeky whistle on his lips.

Winking, he grins at Riehl, then starts banging on the yellowing keys.

"One girl wants to get up early, three quarters before dawn…"

"The Blackberry Song!"[6]

König begins to bellow out the lyrics. His voice is howling and hoarse. Teuscher and Fuchsberger join in, Heenemann and Marjelly follow. Louise hums the melody; she has heard it plenty of times, but she just can't quite grasp the meaning of the lyrics.

Riehl is helpless; he gives them a forced smile and a dismissive wave.

"Didn't quite work out today. Goodbye for now!"

Maßmann has stood up.

"You shouldn't believe everyone who tries to tell on us."

The four policemen hastily clear the bakery.

Martin Harke is clever enough to continue with three or four rougher army songs, and his comrades sing loud enough to be heard throughout the dark, silent Herderstraße, almost until Steinplatz. When Harke finally lowers his hands, Marjelly has tears in her eyes.

"If only all of this excitement would finally come to an end!"

She looks at her belly, which holds a child.

Louise has sat down on Maßmann's lap, cradling her head against her beloved's breast.

Heenemann laughs without concern.

"Thank god we have Lemke."

Maßmann presses a kiss to Louise's forehead and gets up.

"It's time we took the weapons to some cellar; one day they'll be found in here after all."

König props up his head against his hands.

"Who on earth was that pig?"

Fuchsberger laughs. "Don't think too much about it, Napoleon. There are plenty of pigs in Germany. Especially when there are rewards for piggishness."

Heenemann points his thumb toward the ceiling.

"I don't think we'll have to search that hard. That Lewinski guy on the

---

[6] "The Blackberry Song" (*Brombeerlied*) is a German folk and marching song. Its text deals with a young girl going for a walk in the forest, where she meets a young boy who offers her his help in picking blackberries. The girl initially declines his help, but is quite smitten with the looks of the boy. Fast forward nine months and we miraculously find the girl sitting in her garden, holding a baby in her arms.

upper floor wants us out of the house."

And with that, he walks into his baking room. Marjelly screams; she knows that her husband is about to convey his "evening blessings" through the ceiling into Lewinski's apartment using his Luger Parabellum.[7]

---

[7] The Luger Parabellum, or just "Luger," was a popular gun in the early to mid-twentieth century, still renowned for its iconic design. Its name derives from the Latin proverb *"si vis pacem, para bellum"* ("If you wish for peace, prepare for war").

Chapter 2

Four nights later, Karl Maßmann is arrested at the Herderstraße bakery. He is taken to Alexanderplatz, the Berlin police headquarters. The commissar is overly polite and courteous.

"Cigarette, Lieutenant?"

Maßmann declines.

"I can't imagine that you brought me over to smoke cigarettes."

"Well Lieutenant, I don't think that should stop us from having a friendly talk. There certainly is no need for hostility, is there?"

Maßmann smiles disdainfully. He knows this kind of interrogation routine well enough.

"Oh, don't bother!"

The commissar crushes his cigarette against the ashtray and begins to pace nervously around the room. With a slight shrug, Maßmann rises from his chair. The commissar stops right in front of him, examining him with a devious gaze.

"If you won't testify, we'll just question other people. People who are a little more pliant under pressure. Miss Ostade, for example. I think that lady could tell us quite the tale."

Maßmann laughs in the commissar's face. He knows Louise. He can rely on her completely. She would rather bite off her tongue than betray even a single rifle.

"If that was supposed to be a show of strength, it does not exactly inspire much confidence in the state you represent."

This isn't going anywhere. No longer friendly, the commissar's tone becomes matter-of-fact.

"You know that all folkish combat units have been disbanded!"

Maßmann nods politely.

"So what are you doing at that place on Herderstraße?"

"Your policemen had plenty of opportunity to watch. Why are you asking me?"

The commissar has already started a nervous drumming performance on his desk.

Returning to his seat, Maßmann basks in the utter helplessness of this man, tasked with representing the state's power. A state which lacks every single prerequisite for power.

"You seem a bit weary. Would you prefer us to change topics, maybe to something a little more friendly?"

That is too much for the commissar.

"You are here to answer my questions. Nothing more!"

"Please!" Maßmann leisurely crosses his legs, an ironic sneer on his face. "Keep asking!"

Slowly, the commissar begins to lay out his traps.

"You were a member of the German-Folkish Defense League?"[8]

Maßmann nods.

"What was the purpose of your membership? To be clear, I am not at all interested in the statutes of this association. I want to know about your personal convictions, Lieutenant!"

His answer is an almost audaciously disdainful smile.

"You are giving me way too much credit, Commissar."

Then he stands up, steps to the desk, places his hands firmly on the glass surface, and looks straight at the commissar, his eyes narrowed.

"My personal convictions are easily described in just a few words. Germany is sick. And so it must be cured. That is all!"

The commissar nods.

"There is no doubt about that, Lieutenant. But we do need to consider which methods to employ."

Maßmann's voice takes on a commanding tone which doesn't quite fit the situation.

"In times of need, action takes precedence over lengthy considerations.

---

[8] The German-Folkish Defense League (*Deutschvölkischer Schutz- und Trutzbund*) was one of the most influential folkish and anti-Semitic associations in post-war Germany. Officially founded in 1919, the association counted approximately 120,000 members in 1922. The league had some involvement with contemporary right-wing and anti-establishment terrorism, such as the Rathenau murder and the attacks on Matthias Erzberger and Philipp Scheidemann, typically associated with the Organisation Consul. The leagues activities ceased in 1924, with many members gravitating toward the rising NSDAP.

Did you hear the story of the doctors at the sickbed? They argued about methodology until their poor victim finally passed away to meet his maker."

"And your method, Lieutenant? A coup?"

Maßmann knows that he needs to be careful. The commissar's predatory leer is obvious.

"No one is planning a coup. That time is over, Kapp and Lüttwitz[9] made sure of it. But you should remember that we live in a democratic state, Commissar. And in that state, everyone has the right to live by his political convictions, even if you might consider them to be undesirable!"

"Certainly," the other confirms, "Yet the laws of even the most considerate democratic state clearly forbid the use of weapons to turn those political convictions into reality."

"I do not recall any talk of weapons, Commissar."

"Well then, I think it's high time we broached that subject, Lieutenant. We noticed that you and your comrades have been very busy these last few weeks. And not just in Herderstraße, you are also very active in the areas surrounding Berlin. You even took trips as far as Frankfurt!"

Gazing out the window, Maßmann indifferently surveys the disgustingly gray courtyard.

"If you really are that well-informed regarding my life and that of my comrades, you will also know that what we do is perfectly legal. Nothing that a normal, bourgeois club wouldn't do. Namely, excursions. Trips."

A laughing commissar gives the lieutenant a slap on the shoulder.

"Naturally, my good fellow, of course! I almost forgot about your club! 'German-Folkish Wanderers.' Nice name, that. And what a fine badge you came up with!"

With that, he pulls a pin from his pocket, twisting it between his thumb and forefinger. He watches it intently.

"Looks just like the *Pour le Mérite*.[10] Could you tell me the meaning of

---

[9] Walther von Lüttwitz, a Prussian general and Wolfgang Kapp, leader of a national association, were the two key people behind the attempted 1920 coup d'état, commonly known as "Kapp-Putsch" or "Kapp-Lüttwitz-Putsch." Their coup tried to leverage right-wing autocratic elements within the Reichswehr and the newly organized Freikorps to gain control of the German government. It lasted only around four days, from March 13th to March 17th 1920, before being foiled by a general strike, which rendered much of the basic infrastructure such as the postal service, public transit and in some cases, even water and electricity unusable to the newly self-appointed rulers.

[10] The *Pour le Mérite*, first issued in 1740, was one of the highest military decorations in Germany, awarded to officers for exceptional valor. In its military version, the *Pour le Mérite* was awarded for the last time in 1918, among others to German author Ernst Jünger, who was the last living recipient before his death in 1998.

those strange markings?"

"Germanic runes, if you really care that much."

"Also known as a Feme Cross,"[11] smiles the commissar. "You have to admit, that is a rather unusual club badge."

"One shouldn't quarrel about matters of taste, Commissar. My comrades and I just like the way it looks, nothing more."

"The men wearing this Feme Cross happen to be, without exception, revolutionaries, Balts, students from the 'German Student's Federation',[12] malcontents, adventurers. Purely coincidental of course."

Maßmann gives the commissar a kind nod. "Your information really is excellent. But do you mean to imply that this formidable group of German men may not even join a hiking club without immediately being suspected of intending to overthrow this glorious state? Do you want to ban us from going into the woods, pitch a few tents, sing our old songs and breathe in the fresh air? Perhaps Berlin is just a little too putrid for our taste!"

"Quite impressive, Lieutenant! I'm amazed at how quickly your veterans managed to transform into nature-loving citizens. And surely it is nothing more than a temporary relapse into old barbaric habits, when, sitting around a romantic campfire, cursing Reich President Ebert, Member of the Reichstag Erzberger, or prelate Kaas,[13] there also happens to be some target shooting with pistols. People say you've also been throwing hand grenades every now and then. Congratulations on this pleasant club of yours, Lieutenant!"

Maßmann shrugs regretfully.

"If such lapses really did occur, I will of course see to it that they are

---

[11] The Feme Cross is a symbol consisting of an equilateral cross inside a circle, also known as a "sun cross" or "wheel cross." Originally referring to organizations of laymen judges during the Middle Ages, "Feme" became strongly associated with right-wing, anti-establishment terrorism in the Weimar Republic, particularly through the so-called Feme murders. The phenomenon gained larger notoriety in 1925 through a series of press disclosures. There is little clarity about the exact definition and frequency of these murders, as much of the public discussion was based on rumors. Feme is frequently associated with the Organisation Consul's statute of killing traitors to the cause ("*Verräter verfallen der Feme*").

[12] The German Student's Federation (*Deutscher Hochschulring*) was an association of students sympathizing with nationalist and folkish causes. The organization spanned across various traditional fraternities and student organizations.

[13] Friedrich Ebert (SPD), Matthias Erzberger (Zentrum) and Ludwig Kaas (Zentrum) were influential politicians during the early years of the Weimar Republic. In the context of Eggers' novel, they can be seen as examples for establishment figures, administrating the German decline. Ebert continued to occupy the position of Reich president until his early death of septic shock in 1925. Erzberger was murdered by members of Organisation Consul in August 1921. Kaas continued to engage in center-right politics, facilitating Adolf Hitler's rise to power through his support of the 1933 Enabling Act. He died in 1952 in Rome.

remedied. Personally, I fail to see what should be so terrible or even subversive about an old soldier firing a shot from the old pistol that saw him through many years of war."

"I suppose you would have me believe that you founded a religious sect, Lieutenant. Because my sources tell me that your harmless association is also actively engaged in missionary work. And this appears to be the rite by which you introduce new disciples to the mysteries of your cult. But I'm not a man of grand words. Simply put: your German-Folkish Wanderers are openly organizing rifle target practice, training young, inexperienced people to wage war."

Maßmann knows he has to pull himself together. The freedom of his men is at stake, and with it, his only chance in the fight for freedom.

He nods openly.

"You may call it religion if you like. Our faith simply revolves around this desperate race. And if one of my comrades should happen to recruit a friend of his to our association, I cannot and will not do anything against it. If that makes me a subversive, prove it! If you can."

The commissar has difficulties controlling himself. His lips quiver with anger.

"Don't try to trivialize this, Lieutenant. Don't you feel the inferiority of all this commotion you're causing?"

"'Commotion?' Well, maybe that's really all there is to it. Maybe everything you or I or any other human being might do to defend their rights when they are being infringed upon is just that—commotion."

The commissar gives him a dismissing wave.

"I have no desire to get into any philosophical arguments with you. You have been found guilty of founding the German-Folkish Wanderers, a subversive, anti-state organization."

Maßmann rears up against the accusation.

"I demand proof of this supposed subversion. You base your intervention on 'proof' that is poorly construed from all sorts of suspicious factoids and rumors."

"You seriously want to hear the details? Be my guest. I can entertain you with an infinite amount of them."

The commissar takes a nondescript writing pad from his wallet and leafs through the pages.

"We are of course familiar with your club's statutes. As harmless as they come. That is to be expected. Then there is the fact that the marching songs of your supposedly nature-loving wanderers contain death threats against

German statesmen and politicians. Walter Rathenau,[14] for example, is referred to as an 'Elder of Zion.' Erzberger is called a 'Roman gravedigger' and the invectives against Reich president Ebert are simply unspeakable. But I'm sure you will consider all of these to be nothing but harmless lapses by a bunch of temperamental, if somewhat politically awkward, foot soldiers."

"But how do you explain your visits to the Reichswehr?" the commissar slyly adds. "What on earth do you want in Küstrin, Frankfurt, Potsdam and Rathenow? Why do you maintain relations with certain police officers?"

Maßmann weighs his head thoughtfully. "When one has been a soldier for many years, one tends to have comrades who grew close to one's heart in many a difficult hour. And if such comrades should end up finding a home in the Reichswehr or the police, is it really all that absurd to visit them every once in a while to exchange memories and thoughts? Or do you smell dangerous subversion behind any and all comradeship? In that case, you would be well advised to lock away all of Germany's soldiers, veterans and recruits alike."

The commissar perceives his irony.

"Why did you and your fellow conspirators never try to join the Reichswehr yourselves? You would have found everything you needed there. Weapons, comrades, war games, armed excursions to the countryside. Instead, you starve yourselves in utterly civilian occupations, brooding over your dissatisfactions, germ cells of subversion. I fail to understand your reasoning, Lieutenant."

"I'll take your word on that. How could you understand me or even the youngest of my comrades? We simply live in different worlds."

"Express yourself a little more clearly then."

Maßmann takes a deep breath. "Yes, we really do live in different worlds. For if my world were not alien and hostile to you, would you have bothered to have me dragged in here? Would you need to interrogate me if that wasn't the case? You are trying to convict me of subversive activities against the state. That is what your world orders you to do. Because it wants to destroy mine. Maybe it has to destroy it, lest it be destroyed itself. So far, I have done nothing tangible to tear down your world. And so you have no

---

[14] Walter Rathenau was a liberal Jewish industrialist and politician during the early year of the Weimar Republic. Rathenau was accused of collaborating with the Allied governments through his engagement in delivering the reparations demanded from Germany as part of the treaty of Versailles. In 1922, Rathenau was murdered in Berlin by Erwin Kern and Hermann Fischer, members of the Organisation Consul.

legal remedy against me. Unless you take me by force. Earlier in our conversation, we spoke about faith. My faith in this people, Commissar, is my entire world. The state on whose behalf you stand before me did not grow from this faith. It did not arise from folkish law, but from arbitrariness and weakness. That is why it is mendacious through and through. That is why it tries to compensate for a lack of faith through foolish violence."

The commissar wants to interrupt the lieutenant, but his cold eyes force him to remain silent.

"It is not a desire for war games that is reassembling us eternal foot soldiers. If it were, you would be right, we would be well-off joining up with some Reichswehr company. Your state hates the sword; it is hostile to war. Certainly, it makes use of well-paid soldiers. Its desire for security compels it to do so. But your state is so weak, so pathetic and afraid, that it doesn't even trust its paid soldiers. Anxiously it watches the warrior's law resurfacing, even in the small and ultimately harmless Reichswehr. It sees military order and discipline and the path they create for more primal forms of leadership. What happened to your Republican Militia?[15] That ridiculous hermaphrodite fell apart as soon as the petty-bourgeois chaos of 1918 came to an end. Your state needs warriors. Not too many, though, or you would risk a coup. And not too few either, otherwise all those Eastern lice of yours would turn insolent. And that would hardly serve your government's well-known need for a calm bourgeois life. Such are the principles which gave birth to your state. That is why it is jealously guarding its army against conscious, well-informed military leaders, but all-the-more welcoming when it comes to recruiting useless officers and senior positions. Your state wants the army to be harmless, both inside and out."

The excitement has brought beads of sweat to Maßmann's forehead. He awkwardly wipes them away with the back of his hand.

"It did not take me very long to recognize the logic behind your state, Commissar. Do you understand what it means to have lived through the tragedy in the Baltic? If you had understood that, you would have also known that a man's tears are seeds of hatred; hate against everything that is lukewarm and dishonest. Hate against petty-bourgeois politics. And you would also know that I cannot support your state. Have you and your

---

[15] The Republican Militia (*Republikanische Soldatenwehr*) was a short-lived paramilitary organization instituted by Social Democrat politician Otto Wels. Created to uphold peace and order during the immediate post-war period, the organization operated with a strong left-wing bias, partially through its inclusion of troops made up of revolutionary sailors. It rapidly lost relevance after the first few years of the Weimar Republic.

superiors ever bothered to question why there is not a single true warrior to be found in your ranks? Let me explain it to you!"

Maßmann's voice rises in volume. The commissar involuntarily steps closer to his alarm button.

"Your state is as submissive as a devout Christian, praising the rod as it chastises him. But men can only swear allegiance to a state that wields the sword with pride, a state unforgiving unto itself. Nobody dies for a weak state. Especially not for money. But a proud state has no need to recruit men; they voluntarily assemble under its flag. And the honor of a proud state is a greater reward than even the highest pay. You are looking at me in bewilderment, Commissar. I know I cannot convince you. And if I somehow did manage to convince you, you would leave your post before dawn. Perhaps you would join me and my comrades as a lonely German wanderer in search of true men. Searching, not with the lantern of a queer Diogenes or with the fishing net of some religious figure, but with the instinct of a strong man: natural instinct, that infallible compass of the soul."

For a time, the two men remain silent. Maßmann looks downwards, as if ashamed of having profaned his heart's convictions by sharing them with the commissar.

The commissar drums his fingers against the desk. He can feel the lieutenant's superiority towering over him. In some sense he feels reprimanded, humiliated by him. It's a damned thing, having to interrogate someone when what you really want to do is learn from him.

There is a clock on his desk, steadily ticking away, tempering the commissar's thoughts. Gradually, the friendly glimmer vanishes from his eyes.

"Your confession honors you, Lieutenant. Unfortunately, we still haven't made any progress."

Maßmann blushes in anger. He wants to slap himself for his unfiltered speech. What on earth did he think, using such words and imagery? He never talked like that, not even among his comrades. Was that because there was simply no need for it? Because they all shared the same faith? *Now this guy must think me to be some kind of folkish priest*, he thinks. The commissar waits a little before he starts to speak again.

"You admit that you have gathered a group of men to perform a certain task. What is the primary purpose of your organization? Do you have aspirations regarding domestic politics, or do you focus on foreign policy issues? The Baltic, Russia, Poland, France?"

Maßmann cannot help but laugh.

"You really give me far too much credit. Do you honestly think that we would have the leisure to formulate plans? In these crazy times? Maybe if we lived in Australia! You can bet that I would organize a coup d'état. Seize all the power and put men, real men, in charge. A real person for every public office. And then we'd just go on for thirty years, stubbornly and ruthlessly building a true, totalitarian folkish state. But as things stand, Germany doesn't have the luxury of being its own continent. On the contrary, Germany is but a small, very poor section of an overpopulated, racially mixed, disintegrating and utterly confused part of the world— Europe, to be precise. And this Europe has grown old and weary, so old that it is beginning to hate youth and strength. War has rejuvenated Germany. It brought to life certain forces and values that had long been considered obsolete and buried. Pre-war Germany was envied, wartime Germany was feared, and post-war Germany, despite its impotence and internal treachery, is resented. That is why the old Europe is pointing its guns at Germany, keeping its hand on the trigger to open fire as soon as Germany stirs. And you expect me and my friends to bother with plans for foreign policy? As if we were pondering which of our numerous enemies we should attack first? Maybe we'll start by destroying the English on their neat little island, then march on Paris before forming an alliance with Peter Wrangel, the White Czar,[16] to liberate Russia and have it join us as an ally? And while we're already in the East, why not stop by to thank the Poles for their two uprisings in Upper Silesia and other pleasantries, perhaps pay Prague a visit?"

Gradually, Maßmann settles back into a more serious tone.

"No, Commissar, I'm afraid we don't have any foreign policy plans at the moment. Only nations with very reliable swords are able to afford the luxury of a foreign policy. Take this state, for instance. It will never pursue a targeted foreign policy. Rather, it will allow itself to be guided by the whims of each and every neighbor state. So at best, we can expect some whiny hugs-and-kisses politics or breakfast diplomacy. Nothing more will come of it. I am not megalomaniac enough to believe that I can pursue foreign policy goals with a handful of men, despite their fanatical loyalty and bravery. There is only one thing I can do at the moment, and I absolutely will not refrain from doing it. I will be vigilant, watching that

---

[16] Pjotr Nikolajewitsch Wrangel was a Russian general and the last commander of the White Army during the end phase of the Russian Civil War, which lasted from 1917 to 1923. Wrangel was a member of a larger family of Baltic-German nobles.

none of our enemies take advantage of Germany's weakness to invade us, occupy our lands and steal our mines. That is why it is necessary to assemble men who are incorruptible by society's temptations, who fix their burning eyes on our bleeding borders and make sure that nobody is able to disturb Germany's recovery. Can you understand this, Commissar? It really is rather stupid and thoughtless, don't you think? Not putting yourself first, disregarding your own comfort…. Tell me, what exactly is your state trying to accomplish when it persecutes and imprisons the few men who are still willing to defend what little remains of our values? When it tries to break their spirits? What do you think, Commissar, how many men will you find in Germany when you call upon them to die for their state? If you needed men for a suicide mission, serving only the nation's honor? A few thousand, at the very best. And these proud men would die, knowing that they achieved absolutely nothing, except for one thing: the realization of their enemies that Germany has not yet died. Are you smiling, Commissar? I know, I know. I'm relapsing into my preaching tone. Perhaps Germany must first be preached to, before it can once again become holy. Your state cannot preach! I have already told you that it lacks faith. It does not call upon the few. It addresses itself to the many, the way too many; to the masses. To those who want to inherit something from Germany. Who want to become someone; to the opportunists, those rent-seeking economic stallions."

Maßmann's voice is like the roar of a bull.

"When your state calls, Commissar, not a single man will come forward. Just millions of assholes…."

Now the commissar slams his fist on the table.

"Goddamn it, I've had it up to here with you. Are you here as a prosecutor? Who do you think you are?"

The silence returns.

Maßmann stares out the window. His thoughts seem to be far away. Somewhere out in the world. In his world, ruled by men of his blood and spirit.

The commissar nervously leafs through his booklet. His hands are trembling.

"I urge you to limit yourself to information that is strictly factual, Lieutenant. You are unnecessarily complicating your situation."

Maßmann turns around to face the commissar. His eyes still retain the glow of his world, a world which does not belong to the weak and fearful.

"Go ahead!"

"You deny having foreign policy goals. So you are pursuing domestic policies."

Maßmann's voice brims with militarism.

"Remember this, Commissar. I have but one goal and one policy: honor and readiness! Everything else depends on the situation at hand. My comrades and I have adopted a guerilla attitude!"

"Express yourself more clearly!"

"I know of no obligations binding me to a state, save for the ones that stem from honor. However, I consider any revolt against the state to be premature, as long as foreign actors can bring about disaster at a moment's notice. That is why, as has already been mentioned, I watch the border areas, especially the eastern ones. I reject your suspicions of treason as a deliberate misjudgment of our actual realities."

"So what you are saying is that while today you may be ready to bear arms against external enemies, tomorrow those same arms will be turned against the Republic!"

Maßmann remains silent. A peculiar smile is playing around his lips.

The commissar urges him to go on.

"You have said enough, Lieutenant. I understand perfectly why you give lectures on foreign policy. Why you form Freikorps groups in politically disinterested veterans' associations. Why you create organizational cells among folkish students. You are searching for rebels—apparently with some success!"

Maßmann nods. "Rebels! Very well, if that's the word you choose, I won't reject it. But remember that Schill's Black Band was also made up of rebels. And that York's deed was a rebellion as well.[17] Ultimately, it is not a question of the terms used to describe a deed, but of its outcomes."

"Your German-Folkish Wanderers are flying a flag."

A short laugh by Maßmann.

"Yes. We call it the green flag of prophets. Golden swastika on a silken green background. That's our flag."

"The swastika is widely considered to be a subversive symbol."

"Particularly among the Jewish members of your state, I presume," Maßmann sneers. "But calm yourself, we consider the swastika to be more than an anti-Jewish symbol. It is an expression of unity, of a whole. And

---

[17] Ludwig Yorck von Wartenburg was a Prussian military leader in the late eighteenth and early nineteenth century. He initiated the Prussian and ultimately European uprising against Napoleon in 1812, initially without the support of the Prussian king. Ferdinand von Schill was a Freikorps leader, whose Black Band Freikorps fought in the prior Franco-Prussian wars of 1806, 1807 and 1809.

whoever places himself under our swastika commits himself to be whole, a complete person. It symbolizes the sun. The sun, too, is indivisible. Just as life itself is indivisible, so is its symbol. Of course, your state may consider this to be hostile or even dangerous." Maßmann ends his lecture with a dismissive gesture.

"Who is funding you?"

"Funding?"

"Well, who pays for your activities?"

"We do not have any profitable donors. We pay for our own trips. That's what we went into these bourgeois professions for."

"A somewhat novel way to justify your professional duties," the commissar comments with a wry smile.

"It may be novel, but so is the German situation at large."

"Where do you keep your membership lists?"

"So far we have not yet had the time to build up an extensive administrative apparatus. Besides, you seem rather well informed already."

"We have been informed that you are collecting stocks of weapons, particularly hand grenades and machine guns."

Maßmann smiles as obligingly as he possibly can.

"As far as I know the Republic turned in all of its heavy weaponry and destroyed the rest. Even the steel helmets have been smashed. Where would we have gotten those weapons from?"

The commissar angrily chews his lips. There is no point in further questions. Maybe Maßmann's comrades will provide some more useful testimonies. Maybe Louise Ostade will slip up!

"Your arrest warrant remains in force. Try your memory a little more, Lieutenant. Your release date depends on it."

With a polite bow, the commissar rings the bell. Two police officers lead Maßmann back to his cell.

Annoyed, the lieutenant paces up and down the narrow cell, banging his foot against a cot and a foul-smelling bucket. Disgusting! Hopefully he didn't say too much. He blabbered on like an old woman! Or a priest. Yes, exactly like a priest! He had been preaching on and on about some kind of faith.

Him, Lieutenant Maßmann, a preacher! What on earth did the commissar think about that?

Maßmann spends two hours pacing back and forth in his cell, trying to recall every word of the interrogation. Can't forget anything! In two or three hours the interrogation will start all over again. The commissar is smart and cunning, he will try to lure him in, soften him by pointing out his contradictions. He is experienced. If only his comrades won't be careless. Especially Harke and Napoleon, the big talkers. They are quick to get ahead of themselves, and before they know it, he's got them.

Louise?

Maßmann snaps his fingers. Good old Louise! *They won't get anything out of her. I wonder if she's asleep now. Or spending the night at Heenemann's?* Of course she'll be sitting at Heenemann's, practicing interrogation with their comrades.

He cannot help but smile. Good thing that he told them about potential statements in the last few days before the arrest. Louise will do whatever is necessary. His Louise!

He reaches into the small shelf above his cot. It contains two texts. One with the prison rules. Rules of conduct for criminals. "It is forbidden to…"!

Sing and make noise? He starts whistling. A soldier's song from the Baltic. Has it ever been whistled in this cell? Very unlikely! So far, this cell has held petty thieves, tramps, prostitutes, and homosexuals. And they must have been scared shitless. And today, he is an outcast, just like them! With some differences, of course. Separated by gaps, wide enough for a whole world. But this state does not discriminate. It diminishes one's deeds so much that one hardly notices the difference.

Maßmann spits. Despicable, to lock men into this pigsty! He rummages in his pockets until he finds a pencil. Then he scribbles his name onto the prison rules. His full name and title: Karl Maßmann, Lieutenant. Thickly underlined. And now the date. Berlin, the—what day was it again? He counts and laughs. Indeed, January 27th, 1921! January 27th! That's when they used to celebrate the emperor's birthday! *Heil dir im Siegerkranz…*![18] Champagne glasses, pledge of allegiance, hurrah! The emperor's birthday! Has it really been only three years since the last celebration? Can he be certain that it wasn't just a fairy tale? "Once upon a time, three thousand years ago, in a faraway land…"?

A bitter taste in Maßmann's mouth. The emperor! The crown! The empire! When things became serious, when death was testing them for the first time, everything fell apart, just like a ghost. Because death is a matter of pride. And dignity! And a ruler must be man enough to see reality for

---

[18] "*Heil dir im Siegerkranz*" ("Hail to Thee in the Victor's Crown") was the Prussian anthem from 1795 to 1871. In 1871 it became the national anthem of the German Reich. The anthem's text reflects on the privileges and duties of an emperor.

what it is. He mustn't be vain and he mustn't be soft. And he always has to be faithful. Faithful to oneself as well as the few men who deserve loyalty. You can't drop a man like Ludendorff[19] just because a few miserable wretches want you to.

"Fühl in des Thrones Glanz Die hohe Wonne ganz!" What a stupid text. Nothing but lies!

Maßmann spits once again. It was bound to happen. That's why he became a rebel, to remain faithful where monarchs betray their people!

Everywhere in Germany, perhaps at this very hour, patriotic philistines are celebrating! "Hurrah, hurrah, hurrah! We want our emperor back!" Like a child crying for its lost doll. The same doll it threw away on a whim.

What a sad emperor, thinks Maßmann. *When the enemies demanded your extradition, we tried to protect you. One final time, I traveled all across the country to promote the "League for the Protection of Wilhelm II, his life and his freedom." And you had already fled that bleeding, reeling Germany, taking our loyalty for granted.*

Annoyed, he throws the prison rules against the floor.

The second text is the Bible. What a curious combination: Bible and prison rules!

What might be their connection?

"Let's see what the good Lord has to say," Maßmann laughs softly, and randomly opens the scripture.

"And as for those of you who are left, I will send faintness into their hearts."[20]

One of the old Moses verses.

That Jewish god of theirs has done some solid work!

Maßmann thinks of the many sermons he had to endure as a soldier.

A Bible passage for every situation, explained and interpreted just as it suited them. This Jewish book was supposed to answer the serious questions of German men? Pathetic superstitions, born of fear. Miserable cowardice in the face of struggle and fate!

With a jerky movement he closes the black book and throws it back on the shelf. Surely it will serve as a powerful oracle to the criminal that will inherit his cell.

He unhooks the cot from the wall. Easy enough.

But falling asleep is impossible.

---

[19] As part of the Great General Staff, Erich Ludendorff was a leading military figure throughout the second half of World War I. On October 26th, 1918, Ludendorff was formally dismissed by Emperor Wilhelm II.
[20] This passage is taken from Leviticus 26, verse 36.

Chapter 3

Schramm's ballrooms in Wilmersdorf[21] are bustling with activity. A former military band plays the latest Schlager hits. Not quite as modern as the negro bands that have started to appear all over Berlin, but they are loud and choppy enough for even the stiffest dancer to quickly grasp the rhythm.

The mood at Schramm's is good. Lemke is extremely busy hauling in glasses of beer and seltzer. He only got the waiter position a few days ago. It wasn't easy; police constables usually aren't that welcome after their immediate dismissal from the force. No business owner wants to mess with the police. For Lemke, it did not come as a huge surprise when his superior informed him in terse words of the dismissal order.

After all, allowing himself the luxury of his own opinion is not entirely harmless. Anyone with a passion for nonconformity has to be willing to pay for this with a loss of personal benefits and material comfort. And Lemke is man enough not to beg for special favors from fate, providence, God or any other heavenly and earthly authorities. In his opinion, it is almost a matter of course that a man has to face the unforeseen with stoic composure, almost as if he were to give fate an affable slap on the shoulder.

The only things that bothered him were the spiteful words that Riehl muttered on his way out.

"Here you go, miss," he says, putting a bottle of seltzer water in front of one of the all-too-numerous girls populating the dance floors on Sundays. "Pay for it now, so you won't forget about it later on!" Lemke has some kind of phrase for every guest he serves. The girls have taken a liking to this, giving him fiery looks in return. He's a welcome change to their not

---

[21] Wilmersdorf is a district in the southwest of Berlin.

entirely enviable lives, spending long days standing behind counters, talking on the phone or sitting behind the typewriter.

Lemke's smile is mixed with pity. He is not particularly interested in these kinds of girls, who try to cover up their spiritual emptiness with meager frills.

Sure, he could have dozens of willing girls on each of his fingers, if only he wanted to. But ever since his bride's father kicked him out of the house, love hasn't been very high on his list of priorities.

Devil knows, Lemke thinks, *absolutely everything is connected to politics these days, even love.* A police constable is welcomed by a future father-in-law, but a man with political ideas extending beyond a guaranteed pension is thrown out. Along with his love.

Napoleon's rasping voice can be heard from a corner. What's he up to again? The girls are already peeking into the corner with an equal mix of anxiety and curiosity.

Lemke brings over a few mugs of beer. "Cheers, gentlemen!"

Napoleon's head is dark red. "Would you carry off that bourgeois on your tablet already? Have him rinsed out! His soul is filthy, it stinks!"

And with that he starts laying into a stocky man, who angrily fights back.

"Here's what you get for insulting soldiers, you miserable dog!" Napoleon shouts.

Smack! The blows come flying. The table is overturned, girls shriek, beer gushes over the floor. Groups of men form around the two combatants, shouting and inciting them to fight.

Napoleon has grabbed his opponent by the neck. "Hangmen, was it? Murderers and arsonists? Is that what we are? Capitalist mercs?"

Blood runs down his forehead as he speaks. It looks like he received a hefty blow from a beer mug.

With a jerk, Lemke separates the two fighters. He grabs Napoleon's opponent in a well-practiced arm lock and hauls him off to the door with astonishing speed. One more push and this bewildered enemy of soldiers in general and Napoleon in particular finds himself outside the dance hall, under the shade of a lime tree.

The ballroom calms down right away. Martin Harke has seen to it. At Schramm's, Harke has found gainful part-time employment as a dance master. And, as even the most sophisticated dancing aficionados have to admit, he knows his business. Waltzes, foxtrots, red, green, and blue lighting; it affects the mind, particularly when he announces the switch with a few cheeky, cheerful words. Every now and then, the light turns off completely.

And although the complete darkness lasts only for a few seconds, that is plenty of time for happy giggles and a few hearty cries. For the older couples, he inserts a polonaise or a *Rhinelander*[22] every now and then. A great way to lift everyone's spirits.

So far, none of the Republic's sleuths have discovered that revolutionary soldiers are meeting in Schramm's ballrooms, of all places. Prudence through experience!

After Maßmann's arrest, Louise Ostade had insisted on canceling their evening meetings at Heenemann's.

The police fell for it. They were pleased to see the *Landsknecht*[23] gang scattering in all directions. As a result, Louise, Napoleon, Fuchsberger, Lemke, Harke, and Heenemann were only subjected to relatively brief and harmless interrogations. They only kept Heenemann; Lewinski had seen to that.

Around midnight, the men are sitting around the large, rounded corner table, close to the stage.

At first, Napoleon did all the talking. There was plenty to tell, as always. Funny anecdotes from his interrogation, his most recent pranks, audacious plans for the lieutenant's liberation. And of course a wide array of Freikorps fantasies: acts of sabotage, elimination of traitors, particularly at the ministerial level.

Gradually their conversation has become more serious. Marjelly Heenemann needs help.

Harke has found a couple of decent people to deliver bread for her and help out with chores. They happen to be corps students, working for free. Louise helps out with sales behind the counter. They also managed to find a journeyman for the bakery, a friend of Fuchsberger's. He is not exactly a wizard when it comes to pastries, but his army bread is excellent.

At one of these meetings, Felix Teuscher suggested that they form a commercial organization. That was the founding date of the GFDC—the German Folkish Distribution Company.

"GFDC will set you free!" Napoleon boasts.

GFDC can get you anything. Not just parachutes, but also oaken walking sticks, inconspicuous pocket-sized batons, shirts, caps, swastika pins, skull rings, highly sought-after artillery whips, and whatever else the

---

[22] *Rhinelanders* are a type of partner dance, similar to a polka.
[23] *Landsknecht*, a term originally coined to describe German foot-soldiers and mercenaries in the 15th and 16th centuries, was commonly used to describe common soldiers, evoking notions of coarse, rough behavior.

heart may desire. The client base is strictly limited to reliable men. Some deliveries may also include suspicious-looking crates, filled with a little more sensitive hardware. A special offer for particular customers. All GFDC income goes directly to the "clothing fund," for unforeseen situations. They are already up to a few hundred marks.

"Funding for a total German mobilization," Napoleon grins.

"We'll give Marjelly a loan, interest-free," Teuscher decides. "Heenemann won't recognize the place when he returns from the hole. We'll open a first-class cafe for him."

"*Chez Bombe*," Napoleon teases.

Lemke proudly announces that the chef has agreed to purchase all of his bread and rolls from Marjelly, starting tomorrow.

Teuscher comes up with yet another plan.

"We are about thirty men now. If we all agree to work odd jobs one afternoon per week for the clothing fund, we'll be a wealthy club in no time."

With some surprise, Napoleon realizes that he is completely on-board with this idea.

"We'll have to give you the ministry of economic affairs in our soldier state, Teuscher."

Then he bangs on the table, making the glasses dance.

"Boy oh boy, we'll be rich! Hauling suitcases, beating rugs, selling sausages, collecting old paper!"

A laughing Fuchsberger chimes in with his imitation of the Berlin scrap merchants: "Purchase of rags! Bones, paper! Scrap-iron! Beer and wine bottles!"

Napoleon is still amazed.

"Golly, that's a great idea! We could buy anything. Maybe even a tank. I know a spare one, it's sitting around in a shed near Strausberg.[24] They'd sell it to us for three thousand marks. And you can already get a howitzer starting at about a thousand—they're cheaper than machine guns."

Harke nods thoughtfully.

"We'll finally be able to afford false passports as well."

"Well, well, well, I think I know a commissar who'd be very interested in that!"

The men abruptly turn around.

"The lieutenant!"

Yes, it really is the lieutenant!

---

[24] Strausberg is a town in Brandenburg, to the east of Berlin.

Maßmann looks little pale and tired, but his eyes burn with life and passion.

"It wasn't easy to find you." Napoleon emphatically rubs his eyes with the back of his hand.

"Damn you for scaring us like that! Couldn't you have sent us a postcard at least?"

"Does Miss Louise know…?" asks Lemke after a few moments of unbridled joy.

Maßmann shakes his head.

And while the lieutenant is already neck-deep in questions, answers, plans, and ideas, Lemke walks over to the phone for a short, cautious call to the Heenemann bakery.

What the hell.

Maßmann would love to have about eight ears right now. He's trying to process all of their reports, important and harmless alike, both the facts and their gleeful exaggerations.

He is proud of his men! Not a single one of them has failed him. It almost seems like these unexpected incidents—their arrests, dismissals and other harassment—have triggered a special kind of resistance. Only works with real men of course.

He is sorry about Heenemann. That Lewinski prank—shooting at Lewinski's fearful stumbling steps through the bakery's ceiling—will get him a long time in jail. Perhaps a full year.

"We'll be on heightened alert, starting tomorrow," Maßmann announces.

Napoleon almost hauls himself across the table. "Something going on?"

Harke gives him a friendly slap on the shoulder.

"We have witnessed a comet, lad. And they say that it rained blood in Altötting.[25] A clear sign of fate at work. Expect hoof-and-mouth disease, war, smallpox, and bedbugs."

Fuchsberger pretends to be offended as his comrades burst out laughing. "I'll have you know that I'm a Catholic! Don't you dare make fun of my superstitions."

Napoleon claps his hands.

"Bravo, Fuchsberger! Don't let them take away your superstitions. What else is there to laugh about in these strange times?"

---

[25] Altötting is a town in Upper Bavaria, known to pilgrims for its "Shrine of our Lady of Altötting," also known as "The Chapel of Grace."

Maßmann waves dismissively. He's not much in the mood for tomfoolery, and he can tell that Fuchsberger is just waiting to deliver a sermon in his oily priest tone, with rolling eyes and flailing hands.

"So far, we have spent way too much time waiting for chance; from now on, we will work toward it, with a plan. We have to be in those meetings—crash them if we can't help it. The main thing is that new men can find their way to us, every now and then. Do you know what I mean? We have to gather the thinking men around us. The rebels, not the obedient sheep. The unwilling, not the willing."

Teuscher has propped up his elbows on the table and stares at his lieutenant's lips without blinking.

"Veterans are everywhere, even among the communists, not to mention the Social Democrats. If there was such a thing as a soldiers' party, we would have all decent German men on our side."

Napoleon slowly bends his right index finger into a hook.

"But before we can do that, their leaders would have to be redeemed from their sinful bodies. Just like Karl Liebknecht."[26]

Maßmann answers with a serious nod.

"Whoever tries to awaken a people's base instincts shall be killed. Better that one seducer should die than a hundred of his victims."

Slowly, Teuscher rises from his seat.

"You only have to give the order, Karl. Whatever the mission you set before us, we will not bat an eye."

Napoleon rises as well, almost solemnly and extremely embarrassed. Teuscher continues. "You know what we mean. As long as you're leading us, we won't have to worry about the destination."

One after another they rise. Each adds a word, a sentence, a saying to their covenant.

All eyes have turned on them. The other guests are watching the men's table attentively. Some look a little uneasy.

Harke notices.

"Quickly, let's have a song. And stay upright while we sing."

And there's the song already. They've sung that one a lot: in Flanders, at Verdun, in the Baltic, whenever the air was especially thick and stuffy.

"A stream comes running down the mountains, as fresh as wine on ice..."

---

[26] Karl Liebknecht was an influential Jewish intellectual and politician who played important roles during the German November Revolution 1918-1919. He was executed by Freikorps troops on January 15th, 1919.

That's enough to calm down the guests. But of course! It's just a couple of comrades from the war, who can't help but bawl out soldier songs at midnight!

Oh well, they'll overcome those disgusting memories in due time!

Lemke gives Maßmann a tap on the arm.

"Look at the door!"

Good lord! Is it really…

"Louise!"

Maßmann jumps from his seat and a moment later he is already holding the sobbing girl in his arms.

Followed by cheerful "hellos!" from the comrades.

Louise Ostade is here!

Lemke smiles to himself.

He knows how to make a good phone call!

Louise's eyes shine with joy. She doesn't even notice that one cheeky tear running down her face.

"You've returned to me, Karl!"

Then, with trembling fingers, she nestles open her purse and places a pack of papers on the table.

"Please, read it!"

Maßmann leafs through the papers.

"This is great, Louise! Birth certificate, ID from the consulate, even a police record. There's nothing missing."

All of a sudden, he has turned serious, reverently petting Louise's hair.

"Absolutely nothing missing. So we can get married now!"

Napoleon is the first to regain his composure.

"Champagne! GFDC takes the liberty of inviting the young couple and their friends for a little drinking session."

Their glasses keep clinking until the early morning.

The last of the guests has long since left.

Louise has brought a proposal for Karl.

"The consul wanted me to let you know that he could put you up in a bank if you were so inclined."

Maßmann hastily shakes his head.

"I don't have time for offices yet. There are more important things to do for Germany."

Louise nods with devotion.

Karl knows how to do the right thing.

She trusts him completely.

And in two weeks, they will have their wedding!

They couldn't wait even a day longer.

"Woe to you if you take any other pastor but me!" Fuchsberger threatens with a laugh.

Napoleon gives him a rough nudge in the ribs.

"You really think those two will be kneeling in some church?"

Chapter 4

The commissar has a lot of trouble these weeks.

The German-Folkish Wanderers are popping up everywhere. But always by chance, or at least that's what they make it look like. First they're in Adlershof, then in Köpenick.[27] Usually they're causing trouble, and there are lots of brawls. But he can't quite manage to catch the guys in the act. And of course it's impossible to prove that their acts were premeditated.

Again and again, the police commissioner sends over his notes.

All police stations have received secret orders to keep a particularly watchful eye on the Wanderers and to intervene ruthlessly, if necessary.

The Social Democrat leaders are powerless when the Wanderers decide to crash their rallies.

And even the communists cannot quite defend themselves against the swastika-rowdies. Worst of all, these audacious fellows have an eerie way of creating a thoroughly undesirable resonance within the workers' hearts and minds, sometimes even embarrassingly so.

Complaints by Jewish religious communities are piling up. The greater Berlin area is flooded with anti-Jewish posters. Any counter-propaganda is simply useless.

Now even the synagogue doors are being smeared with swastikas. And the paint does not come off. Apparently they were painted using printer's ink.

There have been pogrom-like incidents at Weinmeisterstraße. Jewish

---

[27] Adlershof and Köpenick are two districts in East Berlin. In the early twentieth century, they were largely industrialized, containing various factories and housing complexes for factory workers.

merchants had their stalls knocked over. The Friedrichshain hospital alone is treating about ten Eastern Jews.

Every Sunday, Jews are being beaten up at Kurfürstendamm. There are even brawls in the coffee shops.

The commissar is irritated.

Mentally, he's already signing his transfer orders.

Could all of these incidents really have been instigated by the German-Folkish Wanderers? Impossible—that would mean an avalanche of new recruits!

Chapter 5

The GFDC has set up shop in a four-room apartment on Marburger Straße.

Their sales are above and beyond even Napoleon's wildest dreams. And he is not exactly prone to pessimism either. The swastika pins alone made for about fifteen thousand sales in four weeks.

Mrs. Louise Maßmann has her hands full, keeping the books, answering telephone calls and sending out parcels.

If this continues, they will need to hire an assistant for the next months.

Baker Heenemann comes over in the evening, although he isn't being particularly helpful. He mostly just tells prison stories.

And Louise cannot help but laugh about them, usually in the morning.

Such a *Landser*,[28] that Heenemann fellow! He got lucky once again, spending only five weeks in prison.

All thanks to Lewinski, who got scared by the men's threatening looks and failed to give a coherent testimony in court.

It is hard to describe how pleased Heenemann was when they led him in triumph to his new café.

Crazy with joy. Hell, he was so happy he would have gone back to his cell for another five weeks!

But it's a good thing that he's back, because Marjelly could be due any day now.

A satisfied Teuscher closes the company ledger.

"We have to load the crates headed for Munich by tomorrow, noon at the latest. We'll use the Friedrichsfelde Station this time, just to be safe. Mrs.

---

[28] *Landser* is short for *Landsknecht* and carries the same meaning.

Maßmann, would you please make out the waybills for the Huber cover address? 'Sent from Mayer, Bayrischer Platz.' You know what to do. And then the warning notice: 'Caution! Fragile!'"

Louise nods, quickly jotting down some notes on her writing pad.

"Where do we send the bill?"

"We won't issue one. There will be a courier from the south next week."

Napoleon pokes his head through the door.

"Say, Teuscher, I just got a note from Essen, they have an armored train for sale. Huge deal. Hasn't even been to the front, good as new. We could get it for thirty-five thousand marks."

Teuscher shakes his head in amusement.

"No, no, no. Let's just leave that armored train where it is for now. I'm sure they'll find a use for it soon enough down there. Besides, we'd just get caught if we tried to transport it to Berlin."

Napoleon pouts. "The opportunity of a lifetime. And you just let it slip away. One day you'll be sorry. I'll be sure to remind you."

Louise waves at him. "Oh, don't get upset. After all, you got your tank, the two howitzers, the flamethrowers and twelve heavy machine guns. You big boy!"

"Well!" Napoleon looks mollified. "I'll just go ahead and track down some more of the smaller stuff then."

The telephone rings.

"GFDC here," Louise announces.

Then she smiles.

"Good evening, Karl."

"I'll be with you in half an hour. I'm bringing Heenemann and Harke with me. Please have the other inner circle comrades come to Marburger Straße right away."

"They're already here, except for Lemke and Fuchsberger."

"Even better."

45 minutes later, Maßmann is giving instructions. "There won't be any heckling from our side. We have to lure them out of their foxhole first. Only folkish groups have been invited, so there won't be any brawls."

Napoleon purses his lower lip into a mocking smile, while he emphatically disposes of his artillery whip which had been carefully stowed away under his vest and breeches.

"Not a big fan of these posh meetings. They're pointless; nothing is going to happen."

Maßmann gives him an indifferent nod.

"Who knows? The gentleman looking to speak to us tonight is acting like he's extremely important."

Fuchsberger is suspicious.

"A colonel from Bavaria? I met some very peculiar people down there."

Maßmann checks his watch.

"We have to go. And remember: this is a closed circle, with rather… distinguished guests. You will behave yourselves accordingly!"

The two cabs stop in front of the Fürstenhof Hotel at Potsdamer Platz. There's a crowd of almost eighty gentlemen waiting in one of its elegantly furnished halls. Most of them are clearly recognizable as former military officers.

Louise is the only woman present.

She can feel the men's astonished looks and instinctively snuggles up to Maßmann.

Fuchsberger discreetly points toward a corner.

"Look over there. Four Catholic priests. I smell potential!"

Maßmann gestures them to be quiet.

A bell is swung.

"Gentlemen, may I have your attention!"

A small man in a dark suit has risen from his seat. He looks a little nervous.

"We have asked leading gentlemen of the folkish movement to join us here—insofar as their addresses were available to us—in order to define the intellectual foundations and the aims of our struggle. We hope to establish a working group for this purpose."

"Waste of time," growls Napoleon, "we couldn't attract a dog to our movement with those intellectuals."

A well-meaning, unobtrusive kick from Martin Harke manages to silence Napoleon.

Meanwhile, the gentleman in the dark suit has greeted the Bavarian colonel and given the floor to him.

The colonel's introduction is of no interest to any of the Folkish Wanderers.

This is just ridiculous. Does this guy really think they didn't already know that their poor fatherland was bleeding from a thousand wounds and urgently needed to be saved? Is that why they bothered to come here?

Fuchsberger has put on his Feme Cross, a silent protest.

Harke, Napoleon and Teuscher follow suit.

What an absolute idiot!

Maßmann observes the orator closely.

He does not like this colonel. The man is suspicious, his mannerisms are entirely unpleasant.

Maßmann senses insincerity. This guy is hiding something.

But what?

The speech is slick. Full of self-evident talking points and platitudes.

Surely there is no need to set up a working group for that? Why bother keeping serious men away from more important tasks?

Curious that the priests in the hall use every opportunity to clap and interject their "Bravo!", "Hear, hear!", and similarly approving statements.

Finally, the colonel is getting more concrete. Maßmann breathes a sigh of relief and casts encouraging glances at his comrades.

"Take my word for it, gentlemen," they hear the colonel say, "If we do not fight for a clear domestic policy goal, all of our efforts will have been for nothing. In Munich, we overthrew the Soviet Republic.[29] But what happened afterwards? Nothing! In Berlin, the Spartacists[30] were crushed, Liebknecht himself was shot. But afterwards? Again, nothing! We have to use these opportunities for a great counterattack that will ensure our dominion once and for all!"

"We have to restore the divine order!" Another interjection from the Catholic clergy's corner.

The colonel bows gratefully toward them.

"Indeed, divine order must be restored. And isn't the divine order for Germany ultimately our recently lost monarchy?"

Loud applause rages through the oh-so-distinguished hall.

Maßmann's eyes narrow as he continues to watch the stage.

"I'd like to see this slowpoke try to proclaim that over in Köpenick," Harke says matter-of-factly.

---

[29] The Munich Soviet Republic (*Münchner Räterepublik*) was declared on April 7th 1919 and lasted for about four weeks. Its main objective was to create a socialist republic in the Free State of Bavaria, modeled after Soviet principles. The republic ultimately failed due to military pressure from its opponents, first in the form of paramilitary Freikorps attacks, which were subsequently reinforced by regular army units under the command of the Reich government. The Freikorps Oberland in particular was famously credited with bringing down the Soviet Republic.

[30] The Spartacists were a paramilitary marxist-socialist organization led by Rosa Luxemburg and Karl Liebknecht.

Napoleon is unhappy.

"My precious artillery whip. If only I had it with me now...."

The colonel's satisfaction is palpable.

"The House of Hohenzollern[31] is finished. Unfortunately, that is. But there simply is no way to make up for the imprudences of our last ruler. The people won't have it. But since we have to restore monarchy out of principle, because we have to restore the divine order" —another bow to the clergy—"we'll have to find a different regent for Germany."

His voice swells as he nears the final proclamation.

"Who could be more worthy than a prince of the noblest German blood? Can there be a more valuable man, a nobler personality? In short, who could be more destined to become Emperor of the Germans than Luitpold of Bavaria?"[32]

Again there is applause, although not quite as energetic as before. Except for the clergy, who clap until their hands turn blood-red.

Maßmann's expression has turned into stone. Only his eyes are blazing with a perilous fire. His comrades huddle closer around him.

"You just have to give us the word," Martin Harke wheezes. "One word from you, and we'll tear this whole pigsty apart!"

Maßmann shakes his head.

The colonel has dropped into a chair, visibly exhausted. He uses a silken handkerchief to wipe beads of sweat from his forehead.

The nervous gentleman in the dark suit hastily thanks the speaker. Rushing from word to word, he compliments his wonderful remarks and high patriotic spirit before opening the debate.

It's not a particularly interesting one. Some of the gentlemen make a few timid attempts to defend the House of Hohenzollern, but in the end everyone agrees that a Wittelsbach monarchy[33] was still better than no

---

[31] The House of Hohenzollern was the royal dynasty of Prussia from 1701 onwards. From 1871 to 1918, the title of King of Prussia was attached to that of the German Emperor. Although the Hohenzollern family lost much of its influence with the overthrow of Wilhelm II in 1918, the family with its various branches still exists today.

[32] Eggers is referencing the rivalry between Bavaria and Prussia (which in turn probably originated from the Austria-Prussia rivalry), which has historically manifested itself as either competition for the German crown or Bavarian separatism. To whom exactly Eggers refers with his mention of "Luitpold of Bavaria" is less clear, seeing how the only Luitpold still alive in 1921 was Franz Maria Luitpold von Bayern, who not only was just third in line to the (at this point no longer existent) crown, but also commonly went by "Prince Franz," rather than Luitpold. Considering the rather complicated family tree (the last Bavarian emperor had thirteen children), it is possible that Eggers simply got mixed up.

[33] The Wittelsbach dynasty ruled Bavaria from the mid-fourteenth century until 1918.

monarchy at all. Propagating the monarchist idea had to be the primary objective.

At this point one of the Catholic clergymen rises from his chair: a fat gentleman, with hanging cheeks that extend far below his collar.

His voice is extremely quiet, almost a whisper.

One had to work discreetly, say the things the things people wanted to hear. Criticism was easy, so easy. Thankfully, he declared, the task of the opposition was much easier than that of the government. The right word at the right time: that had always been the secret to success.

"So, you are unhappy, dissatisfied even? Why, yes, unfortunately so! Sad times have taken hold of our beloved people and our fatherland. It wasn't like this in the past. Oh yes, the past! When we had an emperor who took care of everything...."

That was his idea of a good start.

And one shouldn't be afraid to let them rant on about Wilhelm II. After all, he was lost, irredeemably so.

"But haven't you heard of Luitpold? A wonderful man, clearly blessed by God, born to be emperor."

According to the cleric, cleverly weaving those phrases into conversations would be the most effective way to raise Luitpold's popularity in the long term. And when the great day would finally come, that would allow them to save a lot of unnecessary bloodshed.

A courteous smile on his lips and rubbing his hands in satisfaction, the clergyman sits back down.

The colonel and the excited gentleman gratefully shake his hand. Does anyone else wish to speak?

No one seems to be quite in the mood for it. After all, hasn't everything been said already anyway?

Maßmann looks around the room one more time before raising his arm.

"I wish to speak."

A sea of spinning heads.

The excited gentleman hurries to address him.

"Who are you and whom do you represent?"

Maßmann's voice is clear and calm.

"I am Lieutenant Maßmann, speaking on behalf of a military association."

Joyful whispering among the ranks. What a pleasant surprise!

The Bavarian colonel acknowledges Maßmann with a majestic nod and even the fat clergyman rises halfway from his seat to offer a friendly greeting.

After all, soldiers tend to be extremely popular among people with ideas and no power to put them into practice.

Napoleon's feet perform an excited little tap dance.

"Give it to them!"

Maßmann bows in soldierly fashion.

"I have to say, colonel, that your remarks were equally as interesting as the brief explanations of our pastor over here were significant."

Flattered smiles by the ostensibly commended.

Then Maßmann deftly allows for a brief pause.

"You are waiting for your great day, a day that will be favorable to both the Bavarian Royalist Party[34] and the Roman Church. However, both recent and ancient history has shown that days such as these were not exactly blessed days for the German nation. Rather, they have regularly proven to be hours of deepest humiliation and folkish powerlessness."

The listeners' faces take on bewildered expressions.

What is this lieutenant getting at?

The excited gentleman is whispering with the colonel and the clergy corner.

Maßmann's speech is matter-of-factly, as if he were giving a historical lecture on events that happened in the distant past.

"Your hope is to use occasions of domestic unrest, popular uprising, or violent foreign policy events to proclaim another monarchy. And if the working classes should decide to resist this proclamation, you will have them shot with weapons blessed by the Church and wielded by politically inept soldiers. The cowardly bourgeoisie and slow-thinking rabble passing for patriots will be on your side anyway."

"You dare say that to a colonel's face, Lieutenant?!" shrieks tonight's speaker.

The nervous gentleman is performing a series of rather comical leaps as he tries to calm down the increasingly agitated crowd.

The fat clergyman raises his fist at Maßmann, his verbal threats ringing out unheard amidst the general uproar.

With an almost blissful smile, Napoleon has pulled a blackjack from his pocket. He is just about to express his displeasure with the gentlemen in the front row when Harke yanks him back.

---

[34] The Bavarian Royalist Party (*Bayerische Heimat- und Königspartei*) was founded in late 1919, but never formally acknowledge by the Wittelsbach dynasty. It rapidly lost relevance, shedding supporters to other pro-Bavarian movements. It was formally disbanded in 1933.

"Not like that, man. Don't you realize that the lieutenant has much more effective weapons than that?"

Napoleon stops in his tracks, visibly distraught. The small weapon dangles from his right hand, innocent and harmless.

Gradually things quiet down enough for Maßmann to continue.

"Chaos can be brought about quickly, gentlemen. But the cross that the Church hopes to erect on the resulting ruins is a symbol of death. I am well aware that you wouldn't mind another Thirty Years' War[35] to achieve your goals. Yet your goals have nothing, absolutely nothing, in common with those of us who wish to preserve the life of this nation."

The fat clergyman is roaring with rage: "That's the kind of mischief political thought can cause in the brains of soldiers!"

Maßmann dismisses the heckling with a contemptuous wave.

"I know, I know. Until now, politics was Rome's prerogative. That's why the Church did everything in its power to suppress political thought outside its ranks. Do you think we haven't noticed that it is always priests spreading separatist propaganda in all German border areas? That we didn't know why all pulpits proclaim the virtue of hating one's brother? Germany is to remain divided, because brother-wars prevent any real struggle for political power. Try to contain your anger, gentlemen—we too had to learn how to recognize the patterns of history, even as simple soldiers. I will give you the benefit of the doubt, Colonel, and assume that you belong to that group of military men who will never act with historical understanding. Surely you yourself believe that fighting for thrones and altars also means fighting for Germany. You probably do not even realize that you are fighting for a mirage. An illusion that hides not God, but the Devil himself."

The colonel's complexion has turned ashen. His mouth is foaming.

"You dare to sully my faith?"

"What you call faith, Colonel, is nothing but a fantasy implanted into your soul by the agents of a global power. That power is the Church and so you consider it sacred. That fantasy has replaced your truth. In fact, your mind is so thickly veiled that you couldn't even recognize the truth if it hit you square in the face. Your faith was consumed by your religion, and your instinct died in the process."

"I don't get what you're saying; it's just too confused," whines the

---

[35] The Thirty Years' War was a war for dominance over the Holy Roman Empire, lasting from 1618 to 1648, involving a number of European forces such as France, Sweden, the Habsburg Empire, Bavaria, Spain, and many others. Religion, particularly in the aftermath of the European reformation, is widely seen as a significant factor in starting the war.

colonel, utterly helpless.

The nervous gentleman stretches his arms toward Maßmann.

"Well, what kind of authority would you like to establish for the people, then?"

"I cannot serve you with names at this point. All I know is that when the time is come, a man will rise from the very soul of our nation. That time, however, is not for speculators to decide. The goal is Germany. But you do not pursue a goal that is greater than yourself, nothing that would require you to overcome your own limitations. No, you do not serve a goal, gentlemen. You subject ideals to a purpose, and that purpose is your own power. That is why you try to take advantage of absolutely everything. You tolerate the swastika as a camouflage for your cross and its power. You tolerate the folkish terminology and even use it yourself, but only because you want to distract from the Church's political power. You preach about the Fatherland to lure in people based on their natural instincts. I thank you for this evening, gentlemen. It has been more valuable to me than you could possibly have intended."

Accompanied by Louise and his comrades, Maßmann slowly walks toward the door.

A roar of anger and disappointment surges behind them.

"Faithless rebels," the colonel salivates, "Rootless creatures without any tradition!"

"Damned heretics, godless heathens, and swastika idiots," gnashes the fat clergyman.

Already at the door, Napoleon dashes back into the hall, menacingly brandishing his blackjack.

For a brief moment there is a fearful, expectant silence. A chance Napoleon uses to vent his utter contempt and scorn: "You fucking shitheads!"

Chapter 6

Outside, March snow is falling in thick flakes. Louise takes a motorized carriage to Marburger Straße to prepare a pot of hearty mulled wine.

The men opt for walking to help them get over their excitement.

Napoleon is giddy with joy, like a child who, at long last, has been granted a wish that had previously been denied to him. None of his comrades blame him for slipping into his rough Landser tone, even though it wasn't a particularly good fit for the assembly.

They trudge through Tiergarten until they reach Großer Stern.

"I hope you realized the enormity of our fight for freedom, but also its tremendous beauty," Maßmann says before they get into the streetcar.

"Yes," Harke nods thoughtfully, "There are always new forces, new opponents that stand between us and the German goal."

Maßmann shakes his head.

"No. Those are the old forces. They just always appear in new transformations, trying to seize the heart of the nation. Ever since Charles of Franconia disowned the German soul."[36]

Teuscher pauses, then he takes a deep breath.

"We'll have to use the time left to us to study some history."

Napoleon whistles.

"But we'll have to write our own history as well! And who cares if those royal Bavarian thrones and Catholic altars get a little shaky in the process."

---

[36] Charles of Franconia, more commonly known as Charlemagne or Carolus Magnus, is widely known as the first emperor of what would later become the Holy Roman Empire. Charlemagne was the subject of a critical discourse in National Socialist Germany due to his harsh military campaigns against the Saxons, with a particular focus on the Massacre of Verden, in which Charlemagne is believed to have ordered the killing of 4,500 Saxons.

"Bravo!" Lemke says, squeezing his hand.

The men are standing at the front of the streetcar.

There is no more conversation.

Only Heenemann is scratching his head, looking a little embarrassed.

"That kind of talk makes you realize just how stupid you really are!"

Fuchsberger consoles him. "Stupidity can be cured, as long as it's not malicious."

When the comrades arrive at Marburger Straße, the mulled wine is already waiting for them.

Louise fills their glasses, a solemn look on her face.

Then she rises.

"First, Heenemann has to call his wife."

He leaps to the phone.

His head turns bright red.

"Is it really true?"

Then he throws down the receiver and performs a wild dance, shouting and whooping, until his comrades cannot help but doubt his sanity.

Louise raises her glass.

"Two hours ago, Heenemann became the father of a healthy son!"

Heenemann finally regains his composure.

"Me! A son! A soldier boy!"

He strains to think.

"That was just about the time when you settled accounts with those hacks in there!"

Maßmann affirms.

"So my son was born—how can I put this—under a sign. The sign of freedom!" Heenemann continues to rack his brains. Then he looks at his lieutenant, a question on his lips. "Can you tell me the name of a great German who fought against those others? Against the cabals of throne and altar? Who recognized their tricks and traps? Someone who had the courage to poke the wasps' nest and throw fire into it?"

Maßmann rises, so do his comrades.

"Four hundred years ago, there lived one of the greatest Germans:

Ulrich von Hutten![37] A freedom fighter, with an irreconcilable hatred of all dark and parasitic forces in the German lands, an enemy of the crowned and consecrated. He remained a believer, despite dying a miserable death. He fought as a rebel and was victorious in the afterlife. Awakened by his nation's spirit, he would gain immortality in this world of ours. We drink to Ulrich Hutten, the rebel, and to young Ulrich Heenemann, who shall live in his spirit!"

---

[37] Ulrich von Hutten (1488–1523) was a German knight. He is best known for his criticism of the Roman Church, which he believed to have become overly-worldly. He published a number of poems and treatises, some of them against the Catholic Church. Together with Franz von Sickingen, another knight, he declared a short-lived war against the clergy, which ended with Sickingen's death in 1523. Hutten himself fled to Switzerland in order to evade an Imperial Ban (*Reichsacht*) put in place against him, where he died shortly after. Ulrich von Hutten was a common subject of Kurt Eggers, who saw in him an ideal of the virtuous German warrior.

Chapter 7

The first two weeks of March are like a fever, a collective fever in all of Germany. The populace is looking southeast, to Upper Silesia. On March 20th, the people of this hotly disputed country are to decide on a referendum: do they intend to remain part of the German community, bound to the fates of the German nation, or do they want to follow the whispered Polish temptations?

The world is watching Germany intently: how many more tests will this sinister nation endure? Can they really be immune to death?

The news presses work day and night. Rarely have there been such favorable times for political shysters and spiritual poisoners. Billions are set into motion, in various currencies. There are French and Swiss francs, dollars, pounds, rubles, and crowns, not to mention the marks and zlotys. As they appear, they create breaches, buy consciences, kill hearts. World history is turned into a whore, for sale to every traitor who wants to cover his scheming in the beautifying garments of higher political insight.

The shadow of the cross looms large over Upper Silesia. And in its shadow the pestilential rats are burrowing themselves into the country: Who is a good Roman Catholic? Join up with Catholic Poland! Get yourself away from the poisonous breath of the eternal heretic—away from Prussia. By the Black Madonna, think! All of Christianity, think! Didn't the clergy already have to fight against Bismarck for the preservation of Slavic nationality?

And so they rush through the country, prelates and priests alike, slobbering and preaching the break from their German mother. They bless the white Polish eagle and curse the symbols of the German people. Banners advertise the vote on both sides of the border. Their inscriptions are in Polish and German. Promises and threats resound in both languages. Billions of leaflets are being distributed.

The frenzy takes hold of the political speculators. Bets are made, securities and shares rise to dizzying heights, only to plummet to bottomless depths the very next moment. In Paris, London, New York, and Rotterdam, money changers and traders become either filthy rich or destitute.

Meanwhile, the people of Upper Silesia quietly go about their work, behind the plow and in the workshop, above ground and deep within their precious earth. They do not pay much attention to the increasingly nervous propaganda. Farmers and miners know their way. They do not have to ask. They know that it can only be the German way. Every now and then they have a hearty laugh when the propaganda is laid on too thick. As if they didn't know that Germany wasn't a land of milk and honey. But better to be poor in Germany than to be a glutton on the other side.

It would be impertinent to think them stupid enough to believe those lies. As if those on the other side of the border wanted to redeem this country for Poland as an act of charity, out of sheer love for the poor, oppressed German workers and peasants. Seriously? If only there weren't all those damned spies and provocateurs! For honest, harmless Germans, they make life a living hell. Give one of them a good punch in the face and they turn it into an attack on Polish citizens. And if one doesn't defend against them, the press will report that the Germans are welcoming the strangers with open arms!

The patrols of the Inter-Allied Commission[38] are reinforced. The public is becoming increasingly familiar with barbed wire, machine guns, steel helmets, and bayonets. The Germans calmly accept these measures. The others feel safer under show of arms and adjust their behavior accordingly.

In Germany, people are beginning to realize that this time, it's all or nothing. The Reich experiences a wave of rallies. And this time, even the government turns a blind eye, although some of these rallies feel conspicuously nationalistic. It refrains from demanding that the republican flag be displayed.

Clearly the national mood is unavoidable in the context of major foreign policy events!

And so it is alright that there are military bands playing marches and

---

[38] The Inter-Allied Commission was an organization instituted after the end of World War I, tasked with overseeing the execution of the Versailles treaty. Among other stipulations, the Versailles treaty mandated a plebiscite to determine the future ownership of Upper Silesia by either Germany or Poland.

military songs all over the place. That will end soon enough!—or at least that's what the government thinks.

Berlin's train stations are unusually busy until late at night.

Banners call for action. Mobile counseling centers try to support those who are entitled to vote.

Small market stalls are distributing little gifts of love: coffee, chocolate, cocoa, sandwiches, warm sausages.

There are black, white, and red flags, as well as yellow and white ones. The black, red, and gold ones must have been sold out on the first day, because there are none to be seen.[39]

The Red Cross has its hands full looking after the mothers and children.

Through all the noise, all the hustle and bustle, their proud song can be heard again and again:

"*O Germany high in honors….*"[40]

Many travelers have tears in their eyes.

Is this really the year 1921?

The GFDC has set up its stand at the Charlottenburg train station.

This time, the clothing fund of the German-Folkish Wanderers is dedicating its contents exclusively to general charitable purposes.

Louise has lost her head a long time ago. Here's someone asking for cigarettes, over there someone else wants lukewarm milk. And to top it all off, here's a young lad wanting to write a postcard to his bride—with a picture of the victory column, of all things.

Maßmann walks up and down the platform with Harke.

He makes sure that the Wanderers eligible to vote are distributed as evenly as possible along the entire train.

It's a long ride, so people like to talk.

And Maßmann believes that a little political instruction might be in order.

He had a brochure printed at his own expense: *History of the Polish Uprisings in Upper Silesia during 1919 and 1920*.[41]

---

[39] Black, white, and red were the colors of the German Reich until 1918. The flag of Silesia is a bicolor of white and yellow, or silver and gold. The flag of the Weimar Republic was black, red, and gold. After the fall of National Socialist Germany, it became the flag of the Federal Republic of Germany.

[40] "*Oh Deutschland hoch in Ehren*" is a patriotic German song, written in 1859, extolling the virtues of loyalty and endurance.

[41] Upper Silesia's population was a mix of Germans and ethnic Poles. In the aftermath of World War I, this led to a number of violent uprisings by Polish insurgents, causing significant disorder and a number of deaths among the German and Polish populations. Wojciech

It would not be expedient for the police to get hold of this booklet, because its final page happens to list the names of the men and groups who were ideologically and materially interested in the uprisings, in alphabetical order.

Maßmann smiles with satisfaction. His men will start to distribute the brochure after the train has passed Frankfurt. There is no police surveillance on the train between Frankfurt and Breslau.[42]

Suddenly, Harke stops.

"Wasn't that our whistle just now?"

And there it sounds again, for the second time already.

"*Argonnerwald*...."[43]

The two of them discreetly walk toward the station building, where Teuscher and Lemke are waiting on their observation posts.

Lemke, usually calm personified, is quite excited.

"You know who just got in? Our old friend, Constable Riehl!"

"We should get him off the train," says Napoleon, currently engaged on some handyman mission for Louise.

Maßmann waves Lemke over.

"Let's welcome him."

Riehl is surprised and embarrassed.

"Strange meeting you here. What are you doing at the station? You're not Silesian after all?"

"Oh, he's just here to eavesdrop on our people's republican soul," Lemke answers dryly, casting a funny glance at the little black, white and red flag Riehl is holding in his hand.

Riehl is visibly embarrassed, but does not quite dare to throw away the innocent flag.

"You are looking so militaristic today," Maßmann winks as he points to Riehl's buttonhole, which is decorated with the ribbon of the Iron Cross.

"Please let me worry about my own affairs," Riehl growls, "And if you have to know, I'm going to Opole to vote, as a private citizen that is."

Lemke has leapt to Louise's side and returns with a little flag, a small green paper flag with a golden swastika glowing from its center.

"Why don't you take this one as well? Usually we just give it to

---

Korfanty, a former member of the German Reichstag, is widely credited with organizing the uprisings. He was also the head of the Polish plebiscite committee for Upper Silesia.

[42] Breslau is the German name for Wrocław.

[43] "Argonne forest at midnight" (*"Argonnerwald um Mitternacht"*) is a German pioneer song from the first world war.

particularly dear friends of ours."

Riehl gives a good-natured grin. "Well, I can hardly blame that little flag...."

As the train pulls out, Riehl waves from the window for a long time... with both flags.

The vote in Upper Silesia has brought an unexpected success:

707,000 votes have been cast for the German homeland, poor and anemic as it was.

Despite all of its powerful momentum, Poland has only been able to capture 479,000 votes.

The world's excitement has reached the boiling point.

What is going to happen now?

Will this be the final result?

The guards of the Inter-Allied Commission are reinforced once again.

Their rifles are kept loaded, day and night.

Their barbed wire has been electrified.

Almost every Berlin train station has started shipping crates to Upper Silesia on a daily basis.

The GFDC's efforts are almost superhuman at this point.

Chapter 8

The small town of Friedrichshagen near Berlin is preparing for its big day. The well-known folkish orator von Graefe wants to hold a mass rally against Judaism in the brewery's main hall.

A few nights before, thousands of advertising posters have been put up in East Berlin. As a result, there has been a number of serious brawls between the poster columns and Spartacist enemies.

"The east stays red!"

Another series of fierce clashes is happening at the city council.

Democrats and Social Democrats are calling for the speech to be banned in view of the blood that has already been spilled.

The motion does not pass.

In Karlshorst and Köpenick, the reds distribute leaflets, calling for a disruption of the rally.

"The east stays red!"

Tickets for the rally have long been sold out. Hundreds have to be refused entry to the hall, which has been closed off by the police due to overcrowding.

Maßmann has ordered fifty of his men to protect the rally.

They form up into small squads before taking streetcars to the Hirschgarten station.

Their meeting point is a copse between Hirschgarten and Friedrichshagen. The copse is ten minutes removed from the Friedrichshagen *Realgymnasium*,[44] which has been designated as a rallying point in case of any

---

[44] A type of public school in Germany which is no longer in use today, focusing on teaching contemporary foreign languages (as opposed to Latin and Ancient Greek) and natural sciences.

unforeseen incidents. The brewery can be reached in thirteen minutes.

When their squad reaches the hall's front yard, the Kosleck brass band has just finished its musical program. Graefe begins to speak.

Some smaller attempts at heckling are stopped by the listeners themselves.

Maßmann knows that the reds will attack from the outside.

Friedrichshagen is a dangerous place. There have already been some deaths here during the Kapp Putsch.

Barely half an hour has passed when Napoleon and Harke come rushing down Friedrichstraße from the direction of the marketplace.

"About two hundred reds are marching in from the train station."

Maßmann gives his orders.

The men clasp their oak sticks and artillery whips.

The clueless red column approaches.

They are singing the "Internationale."

Maßmann's face has become hard.

He allows the reds to approach until they are about thirty paces away.

Then he shouts: "Halt!"

The column stops abruptly.

Their leader takes a few steps forward.

"What's going on here?"

Maßmann leaps forward.

"You can see that this entrance is occupied. Be reasonable; go back home."

The pack is howling with rage.

"Bloodhounds!" "Labor murderers!"

Maßmann takes a closer look at the red leader.

"You were a soldier once, weren't you?"

His reply is a disdainful shrug.

"That dream is over. And why do you care anyway!?"

The pack starts to move, pushing forward.

"It's only a small bunch!"

"Let's just beat them up!"

Maßmann remains composed.

"We are protecting the rally inside. You have come to break it up. If anything should happen, you will be to blame."

A wave of scorn hits him.

"You're just coming here to provoke the workers, you swastika pigs."

Their leader's voice betrays something like pity.

"Get out of here; we won't hurt you. We just want to tear this place apart."

Then he turns to Maßmann personally.

"Of all the things to do, why do you feel that you have to protect the exploiters? You're a bunch of hopeless romantics."

A man from the pack jumps next to the leader and grabs him by the arm.

"What are you negotiating with those brutes for anyway, comrade? This is a rare opportunity. Let's go lads, finish them off!"

Seconds later, the leader has been pushed aside by his comrades, and like a pack of wolves the reds haul themselves toward the men.

Maßmann fights off three or four guys. Blood flows down his cheek and collects in a warm and sweet pocket in his mouth.

Desperately, the men fight back. Their sticks have been broken. But their whips are proving all the more effective!

Maßmann uses a free moment to survey the situation.

It is looking bad.

His few men are standing in a tight crowd, their backs against the wall.

At least their backs are covered.

Suddenly, he cannot help but smile.

Napoleon!

Whirling around his blackjack, he's cleaning up everyone in his path.

What a brave guy this loudmouth from Berlin has turned out to be!

He has long since thrown away his driver's whip because it just didn't seem effective enough.

There, an outcry!

Lemke has been grabbed by the red leader and thrown to the ground.

With a violent jerk, Maßmann shakes off the two guys who have latched onto him.

"Get Lemke out of there!"

Lemke tries to escape his opponent's choke.

In vain.

His veins threaten to burst.

Lemke feels like his eyes are about to pop out of their sockets any second now.

A knife has fallen from the leader's pocket, almost like a dagger. Lemke has seen it, perceived it with the heightened senses of someone on the brink of death.

With his last bit of strength he taps around for it with his left hand.

He grasps the knife.

A stab!

Blood spurts from the artery in a high arc.

Lemke feels the grip of his opponent loosen.

The pressure eases off of his veins.

His eyes return to their sockets.

Through a veil thick with blood, Lemke can see his opponent staring at him, his eyes widened in amazement.

Staggering, he rises.

Lemke is shaking.

He has to vomit.

He wipes his mouth with his hands.

Blood!

Blood everywhere, wherever he looks, wherever he feels.

The leader lies in front of him in a red puddle.

An unstoppable stream of blood pours from his body, almost as thick as his arm.

For a moment, a terrible silence settles over the fighters, their hearts and hands paralyzed with horror.

Then the reds flee with confused cries. They leave their bleeding leader behind.

The audience in the hall hasn't even noticed the fight. Only a policeman, leaning with his back against the entrance door, has raised his head to listen.

Then he goes out into the front yard.

Maßmann approaches him.

"We have been assaulted. See to it that we get an ambulance. There's a badly injured man outside."

Before the policeman can ask a question or begin to demand their papers, Maßmann has disappeared into the darkness.

The men are waiting at the *Realgymnasium*. It is completely silent. They are still feeling the impact of what has just happened. Again and again, Lemke grasps at his throat. Every now and then he spits. Blood!

His jacket is resting on the fence of the nearby cemetery. When Maßmann arrives, Napoleon shouts: "Attention! The lieutenant!"

Maßmann squeezes their hands one by one, firmly looking every single one of them into the eyes.

"Today was tough. But there is not a single coward among you. My thanks to all of you.

"Lemke!"

Lemke steps to the front. He stands upright, arms bent, just as if they were exercising in the barracks. Maßmann grasps his hand, sticky with blood.

"You have accepted the heaviest of burdens. Carry it with dignity! It is easier to slay an enemy in war than to kill a foe in so-called peacetime."

A wince passes through Lemke's body. Then he tightens up again. Maßmann continues.

"It was combat, man-to-man. You killed in self-defense. You did neither more nor less than I or any of us may have to do tomorrow." Solemnly, Maßmann places his hand on Lemke's blood-crusted shoulder. Then he hands him a yellow envelope.

"Tonight, you will march toward Erkner. You will wake our liaison there and hand him the passport inside of this envelope. Our liaison will finish the passport with your details. From Erkner you will go on to Frankfurt by car. In Frankfurt, you get a ticket to Beuthen. Our liaison in Beuthen will tell you everything else you need to know."

Once again he squeezes his hand.

"I believe we will meet again, Lemke. Soon. In Upper Silesia!"

Slowly he raises his right hand in salute to the old field cap. "Attention! Move out!"

After a few steps, Lemke is swallowed up by the dark night.

Chapter 9

On many houses and uncountable windowsills, flags are set to half-mast.

On April 11th, the newspapers reported the death of Empress Auguste Viktoria.[45]

The people are not just mourning the fate of this sorely afflicted woman; it is more than that. It is a clear expression of dissatisfaction with the weak government ruling Germany.

Editorials of the bourgeois newspapers take the opportunity to draw comparisons between past and present.

The officials are between a rock and a hard place: transferring the body to Germany will give momentum to the nationalist spectrum: a particularly undesirable development at this point. But if they do not grant their permission for the transfer, all hell will break loose. It would be easy for the nationalists to appeal to people's sensibilities in order to deal a new, sensitive blow to the already faltering republic.

Good advice has become extremely rare.

Finally, they reach an agreement. Although the transfer will be approved, under no circumstances will they allow the former emperor to enter German soil.

News of a meeting between the folkish and national movements spreads through the Reich like wildfire. It is to take place in Potsdam, on the day of the empress' funeral.

---

[45] Auguste Viktoria von Schleswig-Holstein-Sonderburg-Augustenburg was the wife of Wilhelm II, the last German emperor. After World War I, the couple went into exile in the Netherlands, where they both died.

Maßmann is on a visit to Ratibor[46] when the news reaches him.

He is sitting in a cafe with some Italian officers, harmlessly talking to them about politics, economics, and the increasingly threatening storm that is gathering on the other side of the border.

Polish attacks in Upper Silesia are happening on an almost hourly basis now. The Polish insurgents seem quite intent on unleashing a new war.

German families are made to endure violent torture. Children are beaten senseless; even helpless old men aren't spared.

A groan goes through the tormented country. Only in the rarest cases do the Germans manage to muster a planned self-defense.

The Polish informers are on their guard and report anyone who might possibly engage in any sort of self-defense to the French occupation force. The very insistent French authorities react by arresting the suspect—for his own safety of course. And whenever a suspicion should prove to be insufficient for an arrest warrant, a commando unit of the insurgents intervenes. The usual result: a few weeks spent at the hospital followed by an inability to work for the same amount of months.

The Italian officers shake their heads.

"We can't help," the captain says, "Protecting civilians is primarily the *Apo's*[47] job."

Maßmann knows that the Italians would like to help. But their hands are completely tied by the French. And the *Apo*, the poll police, contains many Poles, at least fifty percent!

It is a pity that the Italian presence in Upper Silesia is so small!

A larger force would be better, because they clearly appear to be on the side of justice, with the tortured German populace.

The English, too, suddenly seem conspicuously in favor of the Germans.

The Italian captain laughs at this notion.

"After all, England just wants to weaken Germany. You know why? If Germany is strong, England is endangered. Or at least that's what they believe. But if Germany were to die, France would become the strongest country on the continent. And then England would be endangered too. That is why England is looking to prevent Germany's recovery as well as its death."

Maßmann nods.

---

[46] Ratibor is the German name of modern-day Racibórz, a city located in the historical Prussian province of Upper Silesia.
[47] *Apo* is short for *Abstimmungspolizei*, the police force tasked with securing the Upper Silesian referendum.

The Italian is absolutely right!

Then a thought flashes through his mind: back in Berlin, at the Fürstenhof Hotel! Hadn't he spoken of the undermining policies of the Roman Church back then? God knows, England has been an eager disciple of Rome. Protestant England, of all places! But didn't every global policy ultimately have to result in an undermining and dividing of all others?

Perhaps this was the underlying difference between globalist and folkish politics: folkish politics did not seek to live at the expense of other peoples, but were content to unearth and cultivate the powers hidden away in their own soul. Imperialist powers on the other hand could only implement their politics through rape, assault, desecration....

The Italian captain gives him a tap on the arm.

"Don't think too much about it. That is just how English politics work. One should learn from them."

Maßmann shakes his head vigorously.

"No. It would be better if every people recognized themselves and turned folkish. Then this world could finally rid itself of these injustices."

The captain smiles. What an odd German!

He believes Maßmann to be a grain salesman from Breslau, just like he told him.

And after all, one should not expect political insight from a grain salesman.

In front of the cafe a familiar whistle can be heard: *"Argonnerwald...."*

Maßmann says his goodbyes to the elegant Italians.

Outside, he bumps into Lemke, who looks exceedingly well-groomed in his new *Apo* uniform.

"The empress will be buried the day after tomorrow. The funeral is to be followed by a march of the covert folkish combat units."

Maßmann thinks about it for a moment.

"I'm leaving this very evening. It will be good to talk to the comrades again."

Lemke's face lights up.

"Give all of them my best regards. Martin Harke, Heenemann, Teuscher, and especially Napoleon. They should join us soon!"

Maßmann nods.

"How far did you get with the *Apo*?"

"I've found about thirty men. Fanatical Germans."

"Do you think you could get twice that number in two weeks?" Maßmann asks.

Lemke shakes his head.

"I don't believe so. Most *Apo* folks are either politically indifferent or fearful. Not to mention the Poles."

His voice grows softer.

"I feel like I'm being followed. Someone distrusting my papers. I had been at the *Apo* for barely three days when the trouble started."

Maßmann thoughtfully gnaws at his upper lip.

"You have to leave from here. Today. You'll be going to Neiße,[48] dressed as a farmhand. You can put four or five of your men on the train without attracting too much attention. Have the rest of them follow you over the next two days."

Lemke breathes a sigh of relief. Then he has to laugh.

"I never dreamed that one day I would learn to desert with a clear conscience."

"The main thing is never to desert your ideals," Maßmann responds. "In the eyes of the bourgeois, rebellion is something disloyal, something false, equal to, if not worse than, any crime imaginable. We will have to get used to being judged from their perspective. What do those people know about higher loyalty anyway?!"

"Harke has a good term for those people," says Lemke. "He claims that due to their puny nature, they can only see things from below, from the privy perspective so to speak. Where we see war, they see only wounds; where we speak of the great struggle for freedom, they clamor about criminal ventures. In their eyes, I am nothing but a base murderer."

Maßmann squeezes his hand.

"We grow lonely from our deeds. But we also grow great, Lemke. And now farewell. The next set of crates will be headed for Brieg."[49]

---

[48] Neiße is another town in Upper Silesia, located at the Eastern Neiße River and close to Opole.
[49] Brieg is yet another town in Upper Silesia, located on the left bank of the Oder River and close to Opole.

Chapter 10

A thicket of flagpoles has formed in Potsdam. From all over Germany, delegations of patriotic associations, national parties, and folkish organizations have arrived.

Giant wreaths in the colors of the Empire or that of the association have been ordered in all of the flower shops of Potsdam and Berlin as well as all over the Reich.

The empress' funeral is turning into a political spectacle of the highest order.

During the night of April 18th–19th, the access roads to Potsdam are bustling with traffic. Generals, staff officers, princes, and parliamentarians come driving. Workers and farmers follow in carts and old trucks.

Girls' and women's associations, student fraternities and men's associations with ideological, economic, or religious characteristics have sent their delegations as well.

The German-Folkish Wanderers have opted to march down the road from Berlin to Potsdam. They have come with two hundred and fifty men. Today they present a rather strange picture, because Lieutenant Maßmann has allowed the wearing of traditional uniforms. And so there are artillerymen, dragoons, ulans, sailors, infantrymen, and cuirassiers marching in a colorful jumble.

At the head of the procession marches Napoleon, the green silk flag unfurled over his shoulders.

At first he growled and grumbled about them masquerading as some kind of veterans' association, but the lieutenant made it abundantly clear to him that everything is happening for very good reasons. Napoleon is still pondering this question. Does the lieutenant want to deceive government informers? Surely he does, because he certainly isn't the type to try and please the high and mighty.

This night march has a solemn air about it.

The silhouettes of pines are outlined in a deep, threatening black against the gray sky. A dull wind blows over the swaying treetops.

Their singing doesn't quite want to work.

Strange!

Soldiers do not exactly tend to be at a loss for songs.

But this time there are no Landser songs, and no one is much in the mood for patriotic songs—plenty of other groups to sing those.

The men search for a song, giving up again and again. They never make it past the first verse.

Damn it! If only the melancholy would leave them.

Fuchsberger tries to get an echo out of the forest. But it just sounds silly, so he refrains from any further attempts.

Martin Harke begins a song. At last! That song which he had sung so often in the Ypres dugouts.[50]

"*The best of deaths to those who fell, their life laid down against our foes....*"

He sings the first verse alone.

The night wind spreads the song among the troop. Its notes have a clear, hard sound. It feels as if they stand firm above the men, refusing to be blown away.

He recites the second verse, slowly and without hesitation.

Ten, twenty, and then fifty men sing along.

And the third verse is sung by all, with defiance as if they had gone out to grab death himself by his bony limbs.

Mit Trommelklang und Pfeifengetön	*With whistles and with drums*
Manch frommer Held ward begraben,	*Many a hero was laid to rest,*
Auf grüner Heid gefallen schön,	*The finest death, on fields he comes,*
Unsterblichen Ruhm tut er haben.	*Immortal fame shall be his crest.*

---

[50] Ypres is a town in Belgium. During World War I, it was the site of five large-scale battles between German and Allied forces. Depending on the estimation, it is said to have been the site of over one million deaths.

> *Kein schönrer Tod ist in der Welt,* *The best of deaths to those who fell,*
> *Als wer vom Feind erschlagen* *Their life laid down against our foes*
> *Auf grüner Heid, im freien Feld,* *In blooming heath and ruined dell,*
> *Darf nicht hörn groß Wehklagen.* *Stands high above all human woes.*

An owl sweeps over the men on its broad wings.

Heenemann shudders.

An eerie feeling has taken hold of him.

Two hours later, the men have already moved into their quarters. The barracks of the former Guard Corps has taken them in. Their straw sacks have not been aired in a long time, and the straw is old and rotten. Teuscher notes this with a few snide remarks.

The barracks gives off a neglected impression in general. They haven't seen this much dirt in ages, not even during the greatest war-time deprivations.

At five o'clock in the morning their rest is over. They each receive some coffee broth and two dry rolls.

Napoleon is in his element. This black broth is just so versatile! You can use it to clean boots, give a dark shine to uniforms and even polish belt buckles!

At six o'clock in the morning, the men are lined up in front of the New Palace. This is where the funeral procession will pass.

The sun means well on this morning of April 19th.

If only there wasn't this annoying dust everywhere. It settles on flags and helmets, but also tongues and eyes.

Finally the funeral procession arrives. At last.

Maßmann gives the command. Their heads snap to attention. Solemnly, the flag is lowered until the procession has passed, along with the black-veiled horses, the carriage, the coffin, the crown prince, the dukes and princes, clergymen, generals, and officers.

Only once does Maßmann tense up. Ludendorff's erect figure becomes visible. Next to him strides the Field Marshal.[51]

In the afternoon, they march past Ludendorff.

Maßmann arranges for his men to march in between the veterans and non-political associations. Completely inconspicuous. Only their green flag

---

[51] The Field Marshal is Paul von Hindenburg, chief of the German General Staff from 1916 to 1918. Officially in retirement from 1919 to 1925, he would go on to become president of the German Reich from 1925 until his death in 1934.

flutters in the wind, its golden swastika shining brightly.

Ludendorff greets the unit leaders with a handshake. There are too many of them for the commander to engage them in lengthy conversation.

An older major affably squeezes Maßmann's hand.

"Those lads with the funny flag marched well. Traditional club, eh?"

Maßmann gives an obliging bow, smiles and remains silent.

The major did not expect an answer anyway. He has already asked this question plenty of times today and is quite content not having to burden his memory with yet another name.

"Surely you and your men will attend the funeral service tomorrow at the Kaiser Wilhelm Memorial Church? You have more than earned the right today. I'll be in charge of the barrier service. Report to me!"

Maßmann raises his hand to his cap, salutes and returns to his men.

He has no desire to go to church.

Chapter 11

At Krumme Straße in Charlottenburg, right next to the streetcar, there is a small inn.

It is the type of inn Berliners call a "coachmen's pub." This inn is owned by a former Baltic fighter, who ended up with the Independent Social Democratic Party of Germany, or USPD,[52] amidst the ups and downs of the post-war period.

Fully in line with his party affiliation, the innkeeper is bright red and emphasizes his sentiments by wearing a red paper carnation[53] in his buttonhole.

Almost every evening, songs resound across the narrow street. They are political songs, with an entirely unambiguous left-wing bend.

"*We swore it to Karl Liebknecht....*"

The police are not concerned about this pub. They care little about the child-like tantrums of the independents.

At most, a thirsty policeman will stop by to visit every once in a while, with decidedly peaceful intentions. And so the pub is becoming increasingly popular with people who, for one reason or another, are eager to avoid the police.

One of these people is Teuscher. He figured out a while back that this would be a good place to have a glass of wine without any disturbances. What's more, the innkeeper had been part of his Freikorps division in the Baltic. Such connections weigh heavier than party politics.

---

[52] *Unabhängige Sozialdemokratische Partei Deutschlands* in German.
[53] Red carnations are a traditional symbol of socialist movements to this day, typically worn on May 1st (International Workers' Day).

For the innkeeper, beer is beer and money is money, and so he has nothing against Teuscher bringing along some comrades every now and then.

Tonight, Maßmann has invited the comrades of his inner circle to the inn.

A joyful excitement has taken hold of the conspirators.

"Is it really happening?"

"Finally, finally a discharge. Last year's thunderclouds were unbearable."

"Let them come, they'll never beat us."

The room is in high spirits.

Only Maßmann is more serious than usual, his hands playing restlessly with a glass mug.

"We have reliable news that the League of Polish Insurgents will strike in early May. There will be bitter fighting."

Napoleon is right on top of it.

"Just wait until you see how we'll get things going. Once the first shot has been fired, we will force the government into action. Then the great freedom fighting will start! You'll see!"

"You're such an optimist," Maßmann deflects, "But I can already tell you that we will be all alone."

"But the commission——" Napoleon protests.

"They will declare against us. France sets the tone over there."

But nothing can spoil Napoleon's mood.

"Then we'll just take on all of them at once."

Maßmann cannot help but laugh.

"Whatever would we do without you, Napoleon? If we ever get stuck, we'll just send you to negotiate on our behalf."

An exuberant Heenemann places his bulky pistol on the table.

"As long as there's still a bullet in this barrel, no battle is lost. And as long as I'm alive, the whole world can kiss my ass."

"I dunno, it might be an even more charming scene after your death," Napoleon adds, almost automatically.

Maßmann slams his hand on the table.

"Not even laying in a mass grave could stop the two of you from fighting."

Then he unfolds some military maps and informs his faithful followers about the situation.

The innkeeper is surprised at how quiet the billiard room is today.

But that's none of his business!

Maßmann gestures at the map of Germany.

"This state will not get itself involved in a real war, not even in the most terrible of circumstances. It prefers guaranteed servitude over uncertain acts of freedom. It has provided ample proof of its lowly disposition. It did not oppose the Polish-French military convention. Nor did it oppose the London Conference,[54] which brought about the occupation of Düsseldorf, Ruhrort, and Duisburg. Our industrial areas in the west are in enemy hands. On what is Germany to wage its struggle for freedom? The London Conference has seen to it that the last German weapons are being destroyed, and this complete defenselessness of ours is to be used to relieve Germany of its industrial areas to the East.[55] Do you get what this means? Indefinite perpetuation of German impotence!"

Harke spits on the floor.

"The day before yesterday they conducted mass arrests in Upper Silesia. Almost all German leaders have been arrested. Germans have been rendered defenseless under the supervision of the Inter-Allied Commission. And I bet that our government knew this would happen all along."

"There has been a League of Nations for a full year now," sneers Fuchsberger.

"Germany should join as well; then at least they could engage in some polite private criticism. Now that would be progress."

By midnight, the men have talked themselves into a frenzy.

Finally, Maßmann rises.

"Immediately heading to Upper Silesia would just get us arrested right away. The government's henchmen have cast a narrow net—too narrow right now. We have to wait for the enemy offensive. When the tumults break out, we will have a good chance of reaching the combat area without being stopped by the authorities."

Napoleon hangs his head in disappointment.

"I'm just afraid of being too late. By the time we get to Upper Silesia, the others will already have taken care of everything."

---

[54] The London Conference refers to a series of conferences that took place in 1921, with the express purpose of determining the exact amount of reparations to be paid by Germany after World War I. When no agreement could be reached, Allied forces occupied parts of the heavily industrialized German Ruhr area. Large parts of the Ruhr area would be occupied by French troops in subsequent years.

[55] Upper Silesia was another heavily industrialized part of the German Reich, with large coal reservoirs and metallurgic factories.

Maßmann looks at him with a smile.

"An entirely unnecessary worry. Besides, I'm ordering everyone to be on high alert, just to be safe. Starting from the first of May."

"Can't I at least send my tank ahead?" Napoleon begs.

Maßmann is getting annoyed.

"So that the government can get it? We won't be able to come up with tanks and such this time. That single tank wouldn't make a difference anyway."

Napoleon is dumbfounded.

He doesn't know that controls have been tightened over the last few weeks and that a large number of GFDC delivery crates has already fallen into the government's hands.

Chapter 12

In Berlin, the first of May begins with a parade of red flags, in all shades and sizes.

Trucks drive through the city, carrying jeering men and shrieking women. Depending on the street they're in, they either wave to the houses or threaten them with fists.

In the east and north there are clashes with the police. There is a casualty at Beußelstraße.

"Workers of the world, unite!" The banners of class struggle are draped across dirty streets, turning the once sacred spring celebration into a frenzy of fratricide and hatred. Joy turns into noise, enthusiasm into blind rage. Shawm bands parade through the streets. Their music is provocative, demanding. And they seem to know only a single melody, the "Internationale."

The masses trotting behind them sing it again and again, mindlessly, without a care in the world. The constant repetitions are like a worn-out gramophone record: agonizing and merciless.

Only rarely are they interrupted by cheers or "Down!" cries.

Speakers are standing around on street corners and squares, spewing their hatred into the crowd, which gratefully accepts the cheap phrases of these overwhelmingly Jewish characters.

For many, the prospect of a bloody uprising seems to make life more bearable. The dark red of their own blood still seems more joyful than the gray of daily misery.

Wherever a Jew knows how to paint gruesome pictures of vengeance and desolation, the masses pile up, approving his pompous words with furious applause.

Hardly anyone notices that the tales of these Jewish speakers tend to have an eerie similarity with biblical prophecies and revelations.

After the working masses got to know their priests, they no longer read the Bible.

Alcohol consumption increases to a multitude of what is usually drunk on holidays.

The alcohol provides a feeling of power, intoxication, and delight… until the brief stupor gives way to disgust.

But once disgust has constricted the heart, hatred becomes even more compelling. That is why the crowd leaders are almost demanding their people to drink.

Sleazy women incite the men's lower urges by their shrieking, mixed with foul giggles.

Disgust shall give way to utter destruction. And the destruction would not be complete if souls and hearts were left untrampled!

The pub at Krumme Straße is filled almost to the point of bursting. Men with empty, staring eyes, their hair tangled across their faces, scruffy red ties hanging about them, down their water-colored liquor between curses and obscenities. They call it coke. It's cheap and it works.

A few of them are just sitting there with their heads bent over the alcohol-soaked wooden table. Buried in their broad, ruined hands, they ponder the unfathomable folly of their failed lives.

The innkeeper is familiar with these comrades and anxiously takes care that nobody teases them. Not even a crude, comradely slap on the back. He knows their kind. They are wont to roar like animals, ready to indiscriminately pounce on a random bystander the very next moment. To beat him, scratching and biting.

The gramophone gives off its tinny sounds.

A men's choir, accompanied by shawms.

"Max Hölz, you're my *Tovarish*…."[56]

Napoleon and Heenemann are sitting in a smoky corner of the bar.

They are watching the hustle and bustle with utter indifference.

The beer in front of them has long since gone stale.

Today is their first day on high alert, so they refrain from beer and

---

[56] Max Hölz (1889–1933) was a German Communist. In 1921, he was sentenced to life in prison for his involvement in a series of armed communist uprisings and explosive attacks. After an amnesty in 1928, he followed an invitation by Josef Stalin to immigrate to the Soviet Union, where he allegedly drowned in the Oka River. There are speculations as to the degree of a possible involvement on the part of the Soviet secret police.

schnapps.

Besides, the pub's decidedly un-soldierly atmosphere annoys them.

Tovarish, Tovarish![57]

Heenemann grumbles to himself.

"Why do you think they're always calling each other '*Tovarish*'?"

"Because they wish they were Bolsheviks," Napoleon replies. "For us, it's just comrades. After all, we don't get to be Bolsheviks; we just get to beat them up."

Heenemann nods. He is quite satisfied with this information.

One of the wenches has positioned herself in front of them. She is eyeing them up and down, shooting challenging looks from her garishly painted face.

Her skirt doesn't even reach the whore's knee, revealing far more of her revolting legs than one would ever wish for.

"Well, darlings? Not enjoying ourselves, are we?"

The comrades look at her dismissively.

"Oh, no need to be so chaste; mother won't see." She is coming closer to the table.

Cheeky shouts resound from the drunken revelers at a nearby table.

The woman has drawn their attention, and so her attempts to approach the two comrades are accompanied by some pretty unambiguous phrases.

A drunk staggers over, snatches the red carnation from his buttonhole and hands it to the whore.

"For your suitors."

"There you go, sweetheart," she says to Heenemann, as with a sudden twist she drops onto his lap and tries to pin the carnation on him.

That is too much for Heenemann's short temper.

"Get lost, damn you!"

And so the carnation goes flying, tracing a high arc across the bar. The whore receives a nudge and cries out in pain. A second later Heenemann can feel some hot scratches on his face.

"You rascal, you villain!"

Heenemann shakes off the whore, staggering her into the next table. The drunk lunges at him. "That was my carnation, you shithead!"

But an alert Napoleon has placed a foot in his way.

---

[57] *Tovarish* is a Russian term, referring to a comrade or an ally. Typically translated into German as *Genosse*, the term was widely used by socialist parties and associations, in opposition to the more traditional and militaristic term *Kamerad*. Both terms are roughly equivalent to the English "comrade."

In yet another arc, the drunk hits the wall.

And in just under five minutes, the pub has been turned into a pile of rubble.

Heenemann and Napoleon are lucky that the others were way too drunk to reliably tell friends from foes and so they got away with some minor injuries.

At the first aid point in the Charlottenburg train station, the knife thrust in Napoleon's arm is quickly sewn up.

And Heenemann's bruised nose only needs a few stripes of leucoplast.

But Napoleon is desperate.

"What if the lieutenant were to send us a message at the pub now?"

Heenemann's brilliancy comes to their rescue.

"We'll just inconspicuously position ourselves nearby so that we can keep an eye on the pub."

For hours, the two of them are standing under the Wilmersdorfer Straße railway bridge.

No order arrives that night.

Chapter 13

A couple hundred miles to the east, key developments are taking place.

In the night between the first and the second of May, Polish guerrillas are called to the border.

Cheered on by their compatriots, celebrated by the girls, they pin the white eagle to their caps.

Flowers shine from gun muzzles, steel reflects the moonlight.

Songs of Haller's Army[58] resound, sung by soldiers in dashing brown uniforms: a hard sound that cuts through the night.

Their columns are massing at the border.

Marching orders have yet to be given.

But the torch has already met the powder keg.

Some Polish daredevils have commenced their actions. Acts of sabotage have shaken the bourgeois population in German Upper Silesia to their very core. German leaders have long since been incarcerated in the dungeons of the French commission.

With feverish eyes, the Polish volunteers are waiting for Korfanty's orders.

---

[58] Haller's Army, also known as the "Blue Army," was a Polish military contingent created in France in 1917. A volunteer unit, it fought on the western front until the end of the war in 1918 and was subsequently transferred to Poland.

Chapter 14

The Folkish Wanderers have received an invitation to the Spring Festival at the Pichelsberg Seeschloß on an utterly ordinary postcard.

"It should be pointed out that the event may last longer than usual. It is therefore recommended to make provisions for any and all eventualities!"

Among the mass of participants and their festive dress, little attention is paid to a number of boldly uniformed men. Some of them have appeared in old field uniforms, with puttees that have been bleached by Flanders clay. Worn-out army boots, also known as dice boxes, are making an appearance. Modern, broad-checkered breeches and new hunting boots mingle with old uniform jackets.

The hustle and bustle of the party drowns out any individual conversation. Everything is engulfed in cheerful movement.

Shooting galleries have been set up in the garden.

Heenemann and Napoleon are eager to hit all the figurines, burning with enthusiasm. No more than one shot per target. Approving shouts from their comrades accompany each blast and every fallen figure.

Two of the targets are particularly popular. One depicts a fat butcher about to strike at an ox's head with a raised ax.

Heenemann aims the air rifle.

"This one's for Korfanty!"

The ax falls with a bang.

Napoleon aims at a colorful soldier, half-hidden in a sentry box.

"General le Rond!"[59]

Another bang. The soldier moves in front of his sentry box and puts on a tinny drum roll.

Thick crowds are besieging the shooting gallery.

The rifles wander from hand to hand. The gallery owner is quite glad about it, too. He won't have to waste a single advertising word on the idle crowd today.

Martin Harke has met a cute blonde girl. The girl does not hesitate when the young lad invites her for a ride on the swing boat.

She even follows him into the dim haunted house, laughing exuberantly. Only as he tries to kiss her does she put up some resistance.

"Oh, that can wait. Next time."

"Next time?"

Harke wrinkles his nose in mock derision.

"I really don't think you'll be able to wait that long, dear."

Then he snatches the surprised girl to his chest.

In the hall, Maßmann is dancing with Louise, one of those new, modern dances.

Louise's voice trembles.

"You have to take me along, Karl. You can't leave me alone. What am I supposed to do in Germany without you?"

Maßmann cautiously peers left and right.

"Be sensible, Louise. You can't be in the Freikorps. Times are no longer romantic enough for us to afford another Jeanne d'Arc."

Louise snuggles up to him.

"I have shared every hardship with you. I have always been around you, even when you were in prison. At least back then I knew where you were; I could worry about you and wait. But when you join the Freikorps, my door to reality is shut. My cares and concerns can't follow you into those veiled lands. Don't you understand, Karl? All that remains for me is fear: idle fear for your life."

Maßmann tries to laugh. But it doesn't sound real.

"Many women feel the same way you do."

Tears rise in Louise's eyes.

"You are my home, Karl. And I have a right to stay in your world."

---

[59] Henri le Rond was the President of the Inter-Allied Commission in Upper Silesia, responsible for executing the plebiscites that were to decide whether Upper Silesia would remain with Germany or become part of the newly founded Polish state.

Her words become hurried.

"I know how to dress wounds. Who else will be able to care for the wounded? You are responsible for the lives of your comrades."

Maßmann breaks off the dance. Leading Louise through the forest of dancing couples, he heads toward a small table.

"I'll try to get you placed in a hospital close to where we'll fight the invaders."

Squeezing his hand, Louise nods gratefully.

Around ten o'clock, the first groups of men are leaving. They bid farewell to acquaintances and unsuspecting friends, laughing all the while. "Oh, we just want to take a little walk through Grunewald."

Heenemann stands near the dice booth. Marjelly carries tired little Ulrich in her arms. She sobs, stunned by what is about to happen. Her tears fall in thick beads on the child's thin shock of blond hair.

Napoleon has won a bottle of *Korn*.[60] He looks at Heenemann, not quite sure what to do.

"We have to go."

Heenemann pulls himself together.

Softly, his large hand passes over his boy's head. He gives Marjelly a kiss on her forehead.

"Don't worry. I'll come back soon."

At eleven thirty, the Warsaw express train departs from Zoo Station. Night trains to the east are in high demand, so the concourse is as crowded as ever.

The numerous Jewish passengers are shocked and outraged by the inconsiderate ways in which a number of sinewy men are looking to make some room for themselves on the train that has just arrived at the station.

The train has already been very busy at the Charlottenburg station, so that quite a few passengers are beginning to make themselves at home in the aisles.

Today the criminal investigation department seems to be particularly curious. Commissars and assistants are carefully examining the passengers. Every now and then they question one of the men. But all they receive is

---

[60] *Korn* is a distilled alcoholic beverage common in Germany. It is colorless and entirely distilled from cereal grains, with a typical alcohol content of around thirty-two to forty percent.

the regular response that these men are headed to Breslau, for the purpose of taking up agricultural work.

They only manage to arrest one young officer from one of the compartments. He is wearing full uniform.

A woman cries out. Is this a criminal? Perhaps someone with a murder on his conscience?

The arrested man turns pale with anger. Without a word he allows himself to be led away.

Napoleon casts a meaningful glance at Maßmann, who has occupied the window seats with Louise. "Another one of those fellows who haven't had enough war yet."

Maßmann nods. "Yes, those are still around."

The woman shakes her head in disbelief. "War? But we're living in complete peace, aren't we? I am going to Ratibor to see my sister."

A Jew joins the conversation. "Every day now, soldiers are being taken off the train. And they're saying that new riots have broken out in Upper Silesia, over a few paltry border districts." A heavy sigh. "Instead of waiting and letting the government negotiate, the swastika rowdies are now starting to wage a war of their own. They say there have already been dead and wounded."

"Terrible," Napoleon commiserates, as the woman wrings her hands in amazement.

The Jew is obviously pleased at this opportunity to spread some underhanded news.

"After all, those insurgents are in the right here. Who can blame them for wanting to expand Poland's western borders? Germany has so many coal mines: she won't even notice the difference losing a few of them. Still better than starting a new war, which will only bring about new harassment from the Entente. That would just ruin the economy."

He doesn't get to continue, because at that very moment a suitcase in the luggage net above him has started to come loose and tumbles downwards.

A satisfied Napoleon returns the oak walking stick, which he had used to give the suitcase an inconspicuous bump, to his hook.

The Jew roars in pain and presses his hand to his forehead, which is beginning to swell into a fist-sized lump.

"Sometimes there are unforeseen incidents," Napoleon states matter-of-factly.

At the Friedrichstraße train station, another slew of suspiciously military-looking men boards the train.

The Jew is getting nervous. "The police are not paying enough attention. It's so obvious why those people are traveling to the east."

"You really can tell a lot by looking at some people," Maßmann remarks indifferently.

The woman has become anxious. Again and again she tries to reassure herself by asserting that the war is over once and for all.

At the Silesian station, the train pauses for a longer stop.

Maßmann marks their seats as occupied and walks to the platform with Louise and Napoleon in tow.

He receives some inconspicuous waves from the compartments. Everything is fine, all men have been accommodated!

He breathes a sigh of relief.

Suddenly, Heenemann appears in front of them, holding a lanky young lad by the hand.

"That's my nephew. He just followed me from Pichelsberg."

Maßmann examines the boy with amusement.

"So, and what does your mother say to that?"

Blood rushes to the young person's cheeks.

There he stands, scarlet-red and embarrassed.

"It's my last opportunity to become a soldier."

"How old are you, anyway?"

Heenemann stomps his foot in anger.

"That's just the nonsense of it! The brat isn't even sixteen yet."

Maßmann exchanges a glance with Louise. She gives him a happy, affirmative nod.

"Occupation?"

"Got into eleventh grade this Easter."

"We have no use for recruits."

The boy clicks his heels.

"I can shoot. I got a military rifle at home. And I'll get the hang of hand grenades soon enough."

Maßmann gives a bright laugh.

"What's your name, boy?"

"Konrad, Lieutenant. Konrad Ertel."

"Well, if you think your salvation depends on it, go ahead and get on the train, Konrad."

Maßmann pulls a ticket from his pocket and hands it to the boy. "See you in Breslau."

His eyes shining blissfully, Konrad Ertel boards the train. Cursing and shaking his head, uncle Heenemann climbs after him.

"Have all the tickets been distributed?" Maßmann asks over to Napoleon.

"Already issued them in Pichelsberg."

As Maßmann is about to get back on the train, a hand rests on his shoulder.

"Just a moment, Lieutenant."

Maßmann flinches and slowly turns around. Napoleon takes a step back.

"You, Commissar?"

He nods.

"Can't say I'm surprised to find you here."

Louise tries to intervene.

"We are on our honeymoon, Commissar."

"My warmest congratulations," the commissar smiles obligingly, "It's just that Silesia doesn't strike me as a good spot for an idyllic honeymoon right now."

Maßmann shrugs.

"We have desired this moment for a long time!"

A shrill whistle signals the train's imminent departure.

Maßmann offers his arm to Louise and helps her to board the train, following her with a single leap.

The commissar starts to follow him, thinks for a moment, and then waves his hand dismissively.

"You are incorrigible."

Slowly, the train pulls out of the hall.

Maßmann awkwardly wipes the sweat from his forehead.

"He got lucky there," Napoleon grins, securing his revolver. "If he had tried to arrest you, I would have shot him down."

It doesn't take long for the first army songs to ring out into the night.

In the corridors and compartments, men fall into each other's arms.

As the train reaches Frankfurt, a majority of Jewish passengers hurriedly leave the train.

Oddly enough, there are no controls here.

With shining eyes, Maßmann looks into the night. Lightning flashes on the horizon.

There is a thunderstorm over Berlin.

Heenemann has taken the place previously occupied by the Jew. And in the place of the woman headed to Ratibor now sits his nephew Konrad

Ertel, eleventh grade student.

Louise gets up, putting her arms around her husband's neck.

"I wish you all the best for what lies ahead of us, Karl."

Chapter 15

Shortly before Breslau, a huge commotion arises in the penultimate car. Martin Harke has discovered a man in the darkened women's compartment. Naturally, this guy does not seem entirely trustworthy to him.

With a furious scream, he tears open the sliding door, grabs the desperately struggling man by the neck, wrestles with him until he has him in a headlock and finally drags him out into the aisle.

Heads are peeking out from all compartments.

Only the private travelers wrap themselves in their coats, anxiously trying to avoid seeing anything. No one wants to risk a court appearance as a witness in a high-profile trial.

Martin Harke is joined by a couple of men who help him tie up the guy from the women's compartment.

A few minutes later, Maßmann enters the women's compartment, which has been turned into a makeshift prison.

"Who ordered you to sneak onto our train, Officer Riehl?"

A groggy Riehl rises from the bench and tries to stand up straight.

"Nobody sent me here, Lieutenant!"

"I'll smash your teeth in if you lie, you miserable dog!" threatens Napoleon, indignantly waving his fist under his nose.

"Stop it." Maßmann waves him off and gives Riehl a piercing look. "Don't try to fool us, man, tell us the truth!"

Riehl has become very meek.

"It's going to sound strange when I tell you what's going on with me. You won't believe me anyway."

Maßmann nods at him sympathetically.

Riehl takes a deep breath.

"I have a brother-in-law, in Opole. He was with the *Apo*. Some time ago he met Lemke and joined up with him. Now he's written to me that things are happening, and if I were a decent Upper Silesian, I too would come."

He looks at Maßmann, utterly helpless.

"I couldn't just stay at home, Lieutenant!"

"And why are you holed up in the women's compartment if you have a clear conscience?"

Riehl looks at the floor, sheepishly bobbing his feet.

"I didn't want to run into you because I was afraid you'd think me a snitch."

"And we're supposed to just believe you now? All of this stuff you're telling us?"

"My brother-in-law wrote me a letter. I have it with me now," Riehl says, raising his bound hands above his head. "It's in my vest pocket."

At a wave of Maßmann's hand, Harke loosens the bonds. Riehl fumbles in his vest pocket and pulls out the letter.

It is clear to Maßmann that the man isn't lying.

"So how do you imagine the fight is going to go?"

Instinctively, Riehl has folded his broad, short fingers. His voice is trembling, a plea to Maßmann.

"Let me stay with you, Lieutenant. I will not be a disgrace to you."

"This is just ridiculous," Napoleon growls. "First you hunt us down, and when we're finally about to be deployed, you just come along!"

Harke laughs at Maßmann.

"Weird how you always get unexpected allies when the shooting starts."

Maßmann walks down the hallway, lost in thoughts. He looks out the window at the passing landscape. Dusk has set in.

Constable Riehl's story has struck a chord with him.

There's a man, a decent fellow at heart and a good soldier. Becomes a Social Democrat, influenced by his proletarian environment. Signs his name under a Marxist political program that he barely knows. A program developed by a Jew. Remains faithful to this Jew for years, despite having no spiritual connection with him whatsoever. Sacrifices his few pennies to an internationale whose real impact he cannot possibly grasp. And there he is, almost superstitiously waiting for the world to turn into paradise. Until one day reality comes knocking; a warlike reality, awakening his true instincts. And just like that, the Marxist nightmare dissipates…!

As Maßmann returns into the compartment, he can see Napoleon giving Riehl a rough slap on the shoulder before squeezing his hand.

"Let's try to make it work, Riehl."

Riehl grabs Maßmann's hand and won't let go.

"I don't know how to thank you."

Maßmann leaves the compartment, turning around once more as he passes the doorway.

"You will get plenty of opportunity to prove yourself as a German soldier, Riehl!"

Chapter 16

Breslau. Schweidnitzer Straße is packed with people. Particularly noticeable are the droves of young men strolling around, stopping in front of store windows every now and then. The owners of cigar stores, colonial goods stores, and clothing stores are having a field day. But the booksellers can't complain either. The military maps of Upper Silesia have long since been sold out, so automobile maps and even maps for cyclists have to satisfy the demand. Even the demand for books seems to have risen to unusual heights today, although the objects of desire appear to be predominantly single volumes of Nietzsche's works or Herrmann Löns' *Warwolf*.[61]

The fraternities present a peculiar sight. Yesterday's elegant students have put on their breeches and puttees, active and inactive members alike. There is a solemn glow on the young people's faces, and the old student song "Fellows, to battle..."[62] can be heard again and again.

In front of the newspaper stands the crowds are particularly dense. Every bit of news covering the invasions in Upper Silesia is being read out loud, so that even those standing in the background can understand the gravity of the hour.

---

[61] *Warwolf* (*Wehrwolf*) is a 1910 novel dealing with the struggle of the peasantry in the Thirty Years' War (1618-1648). Its author Herrmann Löns (1866-1914) was a German journalist and poet, known for the naturalist themes of his works. At 48 years old, he signed up as a war volunteer and was deployed on the western front against France. Roughly one month into his deployment, Löns was killed in an assault attack on French troops.

[62] "Fellows, to battle" ("*Burschen heraus!*") is a German student song from the nineteenth century. The song's title is a reference to a common seventeenth and eighteenth century phenomenon, in which university students clashed with police officers trying to arrest one of their own.

As the reports mention the devastation and the desperate deaths of a defenseless population, cries and curses rise from the masses.

A young man has climbed onto a newsstand. There he stands, his face flushed with anger, his hair tangled around his forehead.

"Our brothers are dying in Upper Silesia, this very second. And here we stand, inactive, because we are not allowed to join them. Last night, the restricted areas behind Neiße have been closed off. Every train is being searched. Hundreds of volunteers have been thrown into prisons. The government is so weak as to ban our mere resistance against acts of violence. They won't allow the use of the Reichswehr...."

A group of policemen breaks through the crowd. Already they have reached the front of the kiosk. At the last moment the young man jumps to the ground and retreats behind a sympathetic wall of excited listeners.

The situation at Claßenstraße is just as excited. Here, a "counseling center" has been set up. But the only thing this center really knows is the fact that substantial areas of Upper Silesia are already under insurgent control. They have also found plans indicating that the insurrection is to be carried on as far as Breslau. Yet there is complete disagreement as to the measures which should be taken to prevent this.

Maßmann and Louise have just arrived from the train station. Noticing that people seem to be steering clear of any and all responsibility, Maßmann is gripped by a distinct feeling of disgust.

An older major tries to convince him that the only sensible course of action is to wait and see, mustering a remarkable amount of enthusiasm in doing so.

"Without the government's support, all measures are in vain," he says.

"I didn't come here to gain the government's approval," Maßmann responds dryly. "My men and I have come to meet the enemy's advance head-on."

The major does not seem to be comfortable with such military terms.

"We are not there yet, *Lieutenant*"—he cannot refrain from strongly emphasizing the "Lieutenant." "Our local militias have to resist as best they can. That is their right and ultimately a private matter. But any military action is to be carried out by the Reichswehr and therefore is a government matter."

"And what exactly are you here for, anyway?" demands Maßmann.

"We support the self-defense troops, providing help and advice."

"Then help us, please. But with actions, not rhetoric," Maßmann protests, pointing his finger at the numerous posters on the wall. They are glowing with colorful pictures and proclamations, all of them urging German men to do their part to protect the homeland. "Paper has never convinced an enemy."

The major puffs up his chest, wide enough to make his medal buckle pop.

"We are here for self-protection, Lieutenant. Join one of the local brigades in the unoccupied parts of the country. Hold your fire and wait for our instructions. Under no circumstances will we allow any Freikorps adventures. Headquarters has pledged not to abandon our purely defensive character, no matter the cost."

Maßmann's eyes have narrowed once again. Slowly, his right hand strokes Louise's arm. He rises from his seat.

"I don't want to take up any more of your precious time, Major. I believe my men and I are needed somewhere at the front. Where German houses are burning, Major, where German men are dying, and where German women are being raped. Where Germany is perishing under what you and your friends are calling 'defensive character.'"

The Major vehemently protests.

"Your tone is uncalled for; it is unjust. We are doing our duty; you cannot just ignore that. You're coming from Berlin, from the Reich. Leading just a few hundred men who are looking forward to their mission. You have it easy! Much easier than we, who have to account for the welfare of hundreds of thousands."

"I am accounting for the honor of an entire nation," Maßmann hisses through closed teeth. "But that is not something I wish to discuss with you."

On the stairs, Maßmann is approached by a captain, who casts an appraising glance at Louise before awkwardly clearing his throat.

Maßmann smiles.

"No need to be concerned about my wife's presence. She will accompany me to the front."

The captain makes a deep bow in front of Louise.

"My apologies. You are very brave."

Then he squeezes Maßmann's hand.

"I overheard your conversation."

Maßmann turns away as if in pain. "It was characteristic of this time. It has the potential to be a time of greatness, but eagerly wants to remain one of shame."

"I am the quartermaster around these parts," the captain interjects. "Surely there is some way I could help you."

Maßmann considers the offer.

"Can you get me volunteers?"

The captain shakes his head.

"They already have their destinations. Most of them have Silesian leaders, and the student sections have already familiarized themselves with the idea of an enemy incursion a long time ago."

"And what about the members of the militias?"

"Nothing to be done through official channels. The veterans' associations are avoiding decisions because they want to remain apolitical, and the *Stahlhelm*[63] has condemned rash and hopeless enterprises."

Maßmann has a bitter taste in his mouth.

"What do these current border incidents have to do with politics? And how is it possible that they are still dithering when Germany itself is under attack?"

The other returns a meaningful smile.

"Well, you see how it is, comrade. Dare nothing, lose nothing! Besides, there are some groups that prefer to hold their fire simply because reserves are highly valued in decisive hours."

"So they cultivate military tradition," Maßmann growls, "but when it is time for military actions, it turns out that all of this tradition has led to the demise of the living organ."

"I could provide you with some funds," offers the captain.

Maßmann accepts gratefully.

"I still have to buy bandages and medicines."

"I can sell you some surplus army stocks. Low prices."

"Finally a sympathetic breast," Maßmann smiles. "Could you also get me some ammunition for our gun? Field gun 16.[64] I'm thinking mostly of shrapnel and cartridges."

"You expect close combat?"

"The Freikorps fighting will leave us no other choice."

---

[63] The *Stahlhelm* ("Steel Helmet") was a right-wing paramilitary association founded in late 1918. Made up primarily of world war veterans, it was close to the DNVP (*Deutschnationale Volkspartei*), one of the major conservative nationalist parties of the Weimar Republic. It was disbanded in 1935 by decree of Adolf Hitler.

[64] The 7.7cm *Feldkanone 16* was a German field gun primarily employed during World War I. About three thousand units were produced by the Krupp Corporation between 1916 and 1918.

An hour later, a happy Maßmann leaves the unfriendly house in Claßenstraße, Louise on his arm.

After that devastating reception by the major, he has every reason to be satisfied with his encounter with the helpful captain.

Most reassuring is the certainty that he will now have enough money to provide his men with food and pay, at least for the coming four weeks. Not to mention a tractor trailer full of ammunition and equipment that will accompany them to Neiße.

Louise is tired and more than happy to finally get to the hotel Maßmann has chosen for a few urgent meetings.

In the afternoon he orders Teuscher, Harke, and Riehl to join him.

"I have a special assignment for the three of you."

The men stand at attention. Riehl in particular is putting in an effort reminiscent of his days as an eager young recruit.

"We'll be boarding the passenger train to Neiße tonight. The three of you will receive ammunition and equipment from a captain who will be waiting for you in front of this hotel at exactly ten thirty. He will lead you to a barracks, where you will load a tractor trailer and leave tonight at eleven o'clock. Harke will be in the lead, Teuscher will drive the tractor trailer, Riehl will operate the brakes of the trailer."

The men click their heels.

Maßmann looks everyone in the eye.

"A lot depends on this transport getting through. Be careful not to fall into any traps."

Then he shakes Riehl's hand.

"I assigned you to this mission on purpose!"

Chapter 17

As the train enters Neiße, Lemke orders his fifty-five men to present. There they stand, perfectly aligned, their uniforms orderly and clean, their steel helmets tightly fitted. It is quite obvious that Lemke knows how to lead soldiers.

Maßmann is the first to jump onto the platform, thanking Lemke with shining eyes for this welcome. Then he has the men step away.

"Everything ready, Lemke?"

Lemke's hand rises to his cap.

"Weapons and uniforms are in a field barn near the Neiße Bridge; ammunition is stored in a granary. Everything in decent condition."

"And the spirit of your men? They make an excellent impression."

Lemke nods with satisfaction.

"We drilled just like in the old days, and it was a joy to see their enthusiasm."

Maßmann calls Konrad Ertel to him.

"I assign you to the special care of Constable Lemke; he will see to it that your military skills are sufficient for your first great trial under fire."

Konrad Ertel beams.

"I will definitely pass that test, Lieutenant. It's just a pity that my teachers can't see me now."

"Where is Constable Riehl's brother-in-law?!" shouts Maßmann to the group of Lemke's fifty-five men, who have just been surrounded by the Berlin volunteers and are being assailed with all kinds of possible and impossible questions.

A stocky man steps forward, the same good-natured type as Riehl.

"My brother-in-law is not such a bad person, Lieutenant, even if he happens to be a Social Democrat."

"Party politics are behind him now; please try not to remind him. Now he belongs to us. I have accepted him into our corps."

The man's mouth gapes open in amazement.

"Thank you, Lieutenant," he stammers at last, "I'll vouch my neck for my brother-in-law."

Ten minutes later, Maßmann has them line up in front of the station.

The Berliners are now standing right next to the fifty-five.

Maßmann's eyes shine proudly.

By golly, yes, that's a decent corps. Almost three hundred men. And all of them volunteers!

Lemke steps up to him.

"This afternoon at the latest, we have to leave Neiße. Neither your arrival nor our little parade has escaped the spies."

Maßmann spits in the dust.

"I only hope that one day we will get our hands on one of the informers."

Then he gives the order to march.

The fifty-five have brought a new song with them, a song that the Berliners take up with great enthusiasm.

Ihr Sturmsoldaten jung und alt,	*Frontline soldiers young and old,*
Nehmt die Waffen in die Hand.	*To arms with faithful hands.*
Der Insurgent haust fürchterlich	*Insurgent hearts are brute and cold*
Im Oberschlesienland...	*In Upper Silesian lands...*

Louise looks after the men. The words of this simple-minded song, probably made up one of these days in the open field in front of the enemy, grip strangely at her heart.

War einst ein junger Sturmsoldat,	*Once there was a soldier*
Und der war dazu bestimmt,	*Whose destiny was cast*
Daß er sein Weib,	*To leave his wife,*
Sein Kind verlassen muß,	*To leave his child,*
Verlassen muß geschwind...	*To leave them very fast...*

There has to be a cafe near the station, she thinks, *Karl will pick me up from there.*

With a few detours, Lemke leads the men to the Neiße Bridge.

Inside the barn, the uniforms are stacked in neat piles; the rifles have been carefully greased and fitted with muzzle protectors.

The lieutenant's praise is like honey for Lemke's ears; God knows he has had enough work in recent weeks moving the stocks into this barn and getting everything ready for use.

Napoleon has taken over as quartermaster. With a knowledgeable eye, he distributes uniforms, field caps, collars, and steel helmets. But to his extreme chagrin, there are no bayonets. Try as they might, the GFDC daggers cannot be planted on their rifles.

Fuchsberger tries to console him by pointing out that the enemy would probably never get in front of their bayonets anyway.

But Napoleon does not want to be consoled.

"How on earth am I supposed to enjoy even the most beautiful assault without a bayonet?"

Their accoutrement takes them a good two hours.

After another hour, the ammunition from the granary has been distributed. Each man has received three bandoliers and four hand grenades. The rest is loaded onto an ancient passenger car Lemke received as a gift from a local butcher. Four heavy machine guns and a cannon are picked up from a nursery.

Lemke is unhappy that he did not succeed in getting more heavy weapons to Neiße. Most of them fell into the hands of the government's henchmen over the last few days. The freight cars arriving in Neiße had been broken open and robbed of their weapons.

Maßmann calms him down.

"We'll get replacements in due time. Besides, our transport from Breslau should be here soon. I'm sure the three of them will bring us all sorts of surprises."

Napoleon laughs and points toward Konrad Ertel, proudly walking along in an almost-new uniform with a gas mask strapped to it.

"Gee, Konrad, what are you carrying around that trunk for?"

Ertel looks insulted.

"It's against gas attacks, smart-ass."

Napoleon is about to burst out laughing.

"Gas attacks? Gas attacks? I keep hearing gas attacks. Don't you know you signed up for a Freikorps, baby boy?"

Visibly offended, Konrad Ertel throws away his gas mask.

"I thought this was the place to go for some great experiences. And now

I am not even to be offered a lousy gas attack?"

Napoleon has to hold his stomach with laughter.

"Just you wait for the first enemy attack, my boy, maybe then you'll need the gas mask."

Deep-red with anger, Konrad dives into a group of comrades nearby.

He bites his lips in annoyance, vowing to never make such a fool of himself again. *If only we were already under fire,* he thinks, *they'd stop laughing at me then!*

At lunchtime, Lemke has prepared a surprise: a spotlessly clean field kitchen is driven right in front of the barn by a tractor. Amidst the cheering men, Heenemann hands out huge portions of peas and bacon.

Maßmann gives his constable a slap on the shoulder.

"So where did you get the tractor?"

"There's an estate nearby. The tenant has lent it to me for the duration of our fight—must be an optimist!" he adds.

After the meal, Maßmann hands out the first pay: eight marks for each man.

Konrad twists the eight mark bills between his fingers. It is his first self-earned money and he is proud that it is a soldier's wage.

At one o'clock Maßmann sends for Louise.

She hasn't been idle in the meantime, buying iodine, iodoform, absorbent cotton, and gauze bandages at the pharmacy near the market.

At half past one, the men march off.

The tractor trailer from Breslau should have been there by now.

Maßmann has already been looking at his watch more than once. He is rather impatient.

A little more than a mile above Neiße, at the Grottkauer *Chaussee,* [65] he has the men stop and relax.

---

[65] Highway.

Chapter 18

Rifle pyramids are lined up along the road. Heenemann and his nephew Konrad Ertel are standing guard, loaded rifles under their arms.

The men have thrown off their uniforms to take a refreshing dip in the Neiße River.

May has brought about an unusual heat.

Fuchsberger sits in the roadside ditch and plays on an accordion, conjured up by Lemke: wistful soldier tunes of farewell, love, sorrow, and dying on the battlefield.

Maßmann has camped out on a hill under a shady chestnut tree.

The scent of its blossoms is sweet enough to take his breath away.

Next to him sits Louise, large flowering branches in her lap.

Maßmann takes in the strange image and commits it to his heart: there she sits, a proud, brave, young woman among warriors and rifles, unconsciously carrying forth a greeting from another world, hidden in those fragrant, flowering branches: a world of strength, a faraway home to great pagan men and women. And a greeting to those few and courageous warriors this world has left without a home.

With wide eyes, Louise looks toward the blossoming expanse, ripening toward bearing fruit. Her full lips part into a slight, yet utterly happy smile.

"Thank you for letting me stay with you, Karl."

He bends over her slender, delicate hand, kissing it intimately.

The sun shines on the bathing soldiers' naked bodies, as their cheerful shouts extend far beyond the river bed and into the wind, which carries their voices to the east.

A roaring engine can be heard from Bösdorf.

Maßmann jumps up and raises the binoculars to his eyes.

A thick cloud of dust becomes visible.

"That could be our tractor trailer!" Heenemann calls out.

After a while, Maßmann lowers the glass.

"I don't see any trailer."

Excitedly, he hurries toward the *Chaussee*. Louise follows behind him, carefully holding the blossoms to her chest.

The bathing men have noticed that something is happening. The first few of them have already rushed back to the shore and started to dress.

Heenemann releases the safety on his rifle. An excited Konrad fiddles with his gun, trying to follow his example.

When the tractor trailer has come to within thirty yards of them, Maßmann recognizes Felix Teuscher.

He runs toward them with great leaps.

The car brakes, coming to a grinding halt.

Slowly, Harke climbs out of the vehicle, directly followed by Teuscher.

The two of them solemnly raise their hands to their caps.

Maßmann realizes that something must have happened.

They are staring off into the distance; their uniforms show traces of a fight.

And that's when he sees the bullet holes in the car.

In a few moments the car has been surrounded by the returning men.

In a low, somewhat quavering voice, Harke makes his report.

"We waited for the captain, just like you ordered. He picked us up on time and so we drove our tractor trailer toward a barracks, where we loaded our car with a light mortar, including munitions, hand grenades, bullets, gasoline, and benzene, tools and food. We loaded artillery ammunition, flare cartridges, blankets and tent sheets onto the trailer. At midnight, we drove off. Riehl was stationed in the trailer, as per your orders. Shortly before Märzdorf, we suddenly heard shots. A spotlight glared at us. As we hit the brakes, we were jumped by about twenty uniformed men with white armbands who aimed their rifles at us. Their leader ordered us to get out of the car with our hands raised. I shouted at him that this has to be a mistake, that we're German soldiers on our way to the front. He shouted back that the government has ordered them not to allow any soldier or transport to pass through. With that, he jumped on the foot-board and pointed his pistol at my forehead. I pushed him back and his people started shooting at us. Fortunately, Riehl managed to throw a hand grenade. A moment later, they're all laid out flat on ground and Teuscher used the opportunity to drive off at full speed. After the hand grenade incident, we were under heavy fire and followed by another car. Riehl climbed onto the roof of his trailer and tried to keep our pursuers at bay. At the Ohlau marketplace, Riehl got wounded. Headshot. I pulled him over to our car and we had to unhitch the trailer because it was slowing us down too much. Behind Rosenhain, we managed to hide in a somewhat secluded farmhouse to escape the pursuers. The farmer was German and willing to help us out. When we tried to lift Riehl out of the car he was already dead. We then took several hours to get the car back into driving condition. The radiator had been shot through several times, same for the oil tank."

Harke lowers his hand. The report is finished.

The men remain silent, deeply moved by what has been related.

With slow steps, Maßmann walks toward the rear of the car and opens the tarpaulin.

There, carefully bedded on crates of hand grenades, lies the dead Riehl. His face is even and motionless, as if he were asleep. But on his left temple gapes a blood-encrusted hole, about the size of a coin.

At a hint from Maßmann, Heenemann and Konrad approach. The three of them take hold of the dead man, carefully laying him onto a few rifles.

Then, with measured steps, they carry him to the chestnut hill.

Harke, Fuchsberger, Heenemann, and Konrad hold the rifles on which the fallen man rests, as if they were a stretcher.

Maßmann and Louise follow, Maßmann carrying the dead man's rifle and steel helmet. Then, lined up in groups of four, the rest of the men join in.

Silently, four soldiers dig into the earth. One of them is Riehl's brother-in-law.

Tears are falling from his eyes in thick drops. He does not try to fight them. Almost solemnly, he smooths out the edges of the pit with his spade.

Then he stands before Maßmann, looking at him questioningly.

"Should I get a clergyman? We are all Catholics here."

The lieutenant shakes his head.

"He knowingly broke away from his world and grew into ours. And so he also fell as part of this world, where only our law applies."

Maßmann raises his head to the clouds and speaks the poem he has spoken so often, at mass graves and individual funerals, but always in the presence of fallen warriors.

Wenn einer von uns zugrunde geht,	When death takes one of us along,
Zerschossen, zerfetzt vom Eisen,	Shot through, by iron shredded,
Dann rauscht es im Wind,	The winds shall swell,
Der zum Himmel weht,	Filled with praise and song,
Von unserm Singen und Preisen.	Toward the heavens they're headed.
Zunächst mit betenden Schritten leis,	At first, we gather in silence and calm,
Umtreten wir stumm seine Gruft.	Surrounding his grave without words.
Dann klingt hell sein Lied	Then his song resounds bright
— Kein Kyrieleis —	—Without pious psalm—
Das hängt wie ein Schwert in der Luft.	Slashing the sky as with swords.
Wir werfen auf seinen toten Leib	Unto his corpse we lower thus
Viel Blumen und Tannengezweig,	Fir branches and many a flower,
Und beten danach,	We pray afterwards,
Daß er um uns bleib	That he might stay with us,
Und uns den Weg der Ehre zeig.	A guide in our finest hour.
Dann schießen wir die drei Salven ab,	We fire a final salute to the brave,
Dorthin, wo wir Feinde wissen.	Toward our enemy's line.
Drei Salven zum Feind	Three salvos to foes,
Als Gruß aus dem Grab.	A salute from the grave,
Drei Feinde sollen es büßen.	Three souls we shall reap for thine.
Wir klagen drum nicht, wenn einer fällt.	Mourn not those who die in duty,
Ein jeder wird einmal fallen.	Once everyone's time must come.
Die Trommel gerührt!	Now beat on the drum!
Und schön ist die Welt!	Regain the world's beauty!
Auch ich werde einmal fallen.	One day I too will be gone

They gently lay the dead man to rest.

Maßmann has pressed the steel helmet onto his bruised head. Louise steps up to the pit, illuminated by bright streams of sunlight. She throws flowering twigs onto the dead man until his body is covered as if with a bright silken cloth.

Then one after another they step forward, each throwing down a twig, a few leaves, a flower.

Riehl's brother-in-law has hurriedly picked a bouquet from a nearby cornfield, randomly gathering flowers and green stalks of rye.

He lowers the bouquet onto the fallen man's chest. Maßmann speaks only a few words. He knows that all of the men can feel that Riehl's death is a great parable. Why should he speak unnecessary words? His commands resound clear in the afternoon air, their salvos whip out hard against the east.

Silently, the men close up the grave.

A large field stone is rolled onto the grave. Teuscher plays the song of the good comrade, with soul and deep devotion. To the men, the accordion's simple tones seem more powerful and uplifting than the organ hymns of all the churches and cathedrals in the world, mastered by an artist's hand.

The brother-in-law carves large letters into the loose sand beneath the stone.

RIEHL

Tomorrow the sand will be blown away, and the next day the small hill will have disappeared.

But what is bad about dead bodies, if their spirits can sustain the hearts of their comrades?

And so his brother-in-law is the first to sing the song in Riehl's honor. *"Once there was a soldier...."*

As the column starts its march anew, all eyes are clear. Greetings and waves are offered to the hill and its blossoming chestnut tree.

The fresh color has long since returned to Konrad's cheeks. Riehl was the first death he had witnessed in his young life.

On the *Chaussee*, a car approaches them at great speed.

Through the glass window, Maßmann can see that the car is occupied by members of the Inter-Allied Commission. Surely they have been lured in by the salvos. He asks Harke for a hand grenade.

Then he orders his the men to stay behind.

He knows that a well-aimed throw could unleash a world war. That is why he wants to bear the responsibility all on his own.

Slowly, he unseals the handle. The white ball drops down toward him. Flawless conditions.

His steady fingers feel for the string.

He does not take his eyes off the car.

But all of a sudden the car brakes and stops. Two hundred yards in front of him, it reverses and speeds back in the opposite direction.

A sigh of relief swells Maßmann's chest.

Turning around, he sees that all of his men are holding their rifles at the ready.

Even Louise is clutching a Browning.

Chapter 19

On May 15th, the men have taken up quarters in a volunteer camp between Schwesterwitz and Twardawa. Oberglogau is very close. From the east they can hear the noise of skirmishes and small battles, day and night.

A new Freikorps, the "Black Guard," has been formed a few days ago, comprised of the Folkish Wanderers and the men who joined them at Neiße.

Almost wall-to-wall with them, the "Black Band" Freikorps is being formed, led by the intrepid First Lieutenant Bergerhoff—a daredevil of a man, stocky, with dark hair and a flaming gaze.

Maßmann has gotten in the habit of discussing official as well as philosophical and ideological questions with him whenever the two of them travel to Oberglogau for consultations.

Things are not looking good at Oberglogau. The mood is irritable and nervous, and opinions are extremely divided.

The nerves of the old, one-armed general are tense, stretched to the breaking point. He curses the perfidy of this world with a tenacity scarcely seen during the Great War.

Damn it! Things were just different back then.

Sure, they had had to calculate with numbers that were large enough to drive a man insane. In the end though, you always knew where you stood and to whom to turn in times of need. But in this devilish arena nobody knows left from right, with new chasms appearing every single hour. Suddenly, a new abyss. A new trap, a new pitfall. Every hasty step could bring about their ruin. And did anyone want to be responsible for that? In the eyes of world history? Mr. Ebert maybe, the impotent Reich president, rumored to be utterly tired of his office already? Dear God, give it ten years and not a single child will be able to pronounce his name!

The general awkwardly reaches for his handkerchief and dabs at his high, wrinkled forehead, all the way up to the bristle-like white hair.

History written by deeds is a thankless, grueling business! He was the one in charge. He alone would receive their glory or, more likely, their condemnations. Only him, the general.

In front of the castle windows, flowering trees have spread their wide branches.

The general is a great friend of trees and animals.

This disjointed world could be so beautiful, if only the people in it weren't so unbelievably stupid!

The chief of staff enters.

His face is strained, utterly joyless.

He has tucked his monocle between the third and fourth button of his military tunic. In this fatal mood he does not feel like wearing it.

The general looks at him good-naturedly.

"Well, old boy? Trouble again?"

The chief of staff makes a dismissive hand gesture.

"Is there anything but trouble in this country?"

Then he becomes serious, unfolds his folder, and stands at attention.

"News from the front is growing less favorable by the day. The lack of ammunition is having an increasingly demoralizing effect. Without a last minute miracle, we must fear that the insurgents will remain victorious. They are receiving new supplies on an almost hourly basis and are steadily gaining in rigor and striking power."

"The Prussians can't be shooting that fast, can they?"

The chief of staff steps up to the map, covering the area with hasty movements of his hands.

"In the industrialized cities, the insurgents are still met with fierce resistance. Of course, this is partly due to the fact that the insurgents dare not engage in large-scale street fighting in the face of the Inter-Allied occupation forces.

"In Ratibor, the Italians have left about twenty dead so that the injustice to Germany would not be all too obvious. Also, the working class is fanatically German and has a remarkable talent for carrying out acts of sabotage. But the corner between Groß-Strehlitz and Slawentzitz is looking very precarious...."

He punctuates the sentence with a blow to the table.

The general looks at his chief of staff, not betraying any emotion.

"I don't consider the situation to be quite so hopeless. After all, you have to remember that this is the very corner in which the insurgents' advance has been stalled, if not completely stopped, ever since May 6th."

Another blow to the table.

"The individual German villages have turned into small fortresses, with heavy static battles being fought for them. But even the bravest of defenders will get tired if he has no certainty of relief or reinforcement. That is the disadvantage of every defensive struggle. And in our case, the circumstances are even more devastating, because relief is no longer seen as uncertain, but outright hopeless."

The general winces.

"Do you mean to say that you expect imminent disaster?"

"The insurgents are fighting with heightened courage and ruthlessness." The Chief of Staff stresses every single word. "They do so because there is an enthusiastic nation behind them which not only rejoices at every village they conquer, but also sends them new volunteers, war material, and money on a daily basis. They have formed a number of excellent storm troops, led by former German officers."

There is a knock at the door.

An orderly enters and announces the arrival of some Freikorps leaders.

The general frowns.

"Those pests again."

Then he waves.

"Let 'em come in!"

And turning to his chief of staff: "Temperament may win you assaults, but political battles are fought with cool composure and mathematical reasoning."

Two minutes later, the Freikorps leaders have entered the room. Maßmann, Bergerhoff, the young daredevil commander von Eicken, the leader of Storm Commando Heinz, as well as the defender of Gogolin, that little town on the other side of the Oder which has become all-important in its resistance against furious insurgent attacks. They are accompanied by another young, extremely tall officer. He has just arrived and the others barely seem to know who he is.

The general is polite and amiable as always when he is mentally preparing to settle disagreements.

He is no friend of vicious clashes and prefers diplomatic settlements whenever possible.

At a gesture of his, the chief of staff passes around cigarettes and cigars. "Well, gentlemen?"

Maßmann fiddles with the map, pointing to the flags indicating the current state of the front lines.

"If the insurgents decided to advance through Leschnitz-Krappitz now, they would be able to seal off the entire industrial area and do whatever they please with it."

The general waves at him, smiling. "If, if! But you're still here as well, aren't you gentlemen?"

Maßmann bows. "According to my information, the insurgents are to receive a tremendous amount of reinforcements, in fourteen days at the latest. They will be able to simply flood the whole country."

"I have received that information as well, but I don't quite believe in it," the general says with deliberate indifference.

Von Eicken is irritated. "You didn't believe that the insurgents would develop serious fighting skills, either. Please have a look at our casualty lists; those should be more convincing than your theoretical considerations."

"Alright, alright, Mr. von Eicken." One could get the impression of a father placating his all-too-impetuous son. "I know that your men in particular are accomplishing unheard-of feats. It goes without saying that your losses are particularly high as well."

"All of this would be bearable," Gogolin's defender grumbles, "If we just had a handful of reserves, so at least they could boost our morale. But as things stand, we are just bleeding ourselves dry in those daily skirmishes. Many of the men have barely had any sleep for weeks now. The insurgents have it a thousand times easier; they are the aggressors and can take rest days whenever they please. We have to be on guard day and night."

The general rolls his eyes. One could get the impression that he's making a little fun of the young hotheads.

"I'm telling you, this will stop, gentlemen. You just have to have to be disciplined enough to wait. I understand that you have yet to grow accustomed to this necessary deceleration. But believe me, I am cultivating highly favorable negotiations with the Inter-Allied Commission as we speak. If this continues, we will be in a position to stage an intervention against the insurgents."

Maßmann laughs defiantly.

"Very impressive, General! If you would manage to bring in, let's say,

General le Rond as a Freikorps leader on our side, I would voluntarily relinquish my command."

The general's face remains stoic.

"My intentions are not quite that ridiculous. I only intend to spare our tormented fatherland new wounds.

"If we can get the Inter-Allied Commission to grudgingly concede that we really have maintained discipline through clenched teeth and stood at attention despite every conceivable provocation and harassment, they will have to give us permission to counterattack eventually."

"Do you think they will also give us permission to win in open battle?" Gogolin asks, his sarcasm more than palpable.

The leader of Storm Commando Heinz nods in approval. "A German victory would reestablish Germany's honor, General. An atonement for 1918, morally and spiritually. For all the world to see. Do you really think that the Entente would allow that? After sending us to Versailles? With honor comes prestige, and a nation's dignity is also its power. The Entente leaders would be fools if they didn't do their utmost to keep us alive, but powerless. Always on the ground."

The general fumbles with his collar. "I am neither a dreamer nor an ivory tower strategist. You can take my word for that, gentlemen. Rather, I would insist that I am the greatest political realist in this very room."

Maßmann clears his throat. "By 'realpolitik,' we do not mean a mere appreciation of the circumstances at hand, but also the use of any and all powers at our disposal to force these very circumstances to comply with the law of our will."

For just a second one can observe an angry wrinkle on the general's forehead. But he immediately regains his composure.

"Thank you for your kind instructions. But perhaps you will be so good as to provide me with some more actionable suggestions. Up till now, you have limited yourself almost exclusively to reproaches against me—although I'm sure they were well intentioned."

Maßmann glances at his comrades. "If we throw back the insurgents, let's say, across the Slaventzitz-Tost-Sacharsowitz line, we'll be able to control the entire industrial area and clean it out completely. But that is only possible with a lightning-fast deployment of all available troops."

"Well then," the general hastily interjects, "That sounds just wonderful. But in reality, you are taking potshots at a powder keg. Please imagine for just a second what it would mean if your attack was repulsed, if your troops were annihilated."

Maßmann shakes his head.

"That is possible, of course. But regardless of the outcome of this particular enterprise, however reckless and even hopeless it may turn out to be, we still achieve something: namely the fact that the insurgents will become more cautious in their attacks. Also, the Entente powers will have to consider these unpredictable outbursts on the part of Germany in their future decisions."

"We are being treated with contempt," interjects Gogolin. "It is intolerable. I have read Polish newspapers which have already begun to make fun of German inaction. They claim that the German soldier is a coward, only kept to his flag by a great deal of pressure."

"Very true," von Eicken nods, "Count Oppersdorf's black car is driving around completely unconcerned, distributing enemy leaflets far beyond the front lines. And right under our soldiers' noses. No wonder they are laughing at us."

The chief of staff whistles between his teeth. "At least we caught the young count."

"So what?" growls Gogolin. "The young count only refers to his father. And we can't get his father because we aren't free in our actions."

The general shakes his head regretfully. "And to think that the young count once was a Prussian guard officer...."

"Then you can gauge what our enemies are capable of." Maßmann continues his sentence: "The former Germans have become our most dangerous enemies."

The unknown officer has risen from his seat and stepped to the map. "If you ask me, the greatest blow against the insurgents would be if we snatched Annaberg from them."

The general's mouth has opened in amazement. "Annaberg? That is beyond naïve."

The other Freikorps leaders are somewhat surprised as well.

Von Eicken laughs softly to himself.

"How often do you think I've looked over at Annaberg, wishing we could just plant our flag on the church steeple?"

The general has composed himself.

"What on earth are you thinking? Don't you know that Annaberg has been reinforced into a key position, with every hill surrounding it turned into a fort? Do you want to lead your men into certain death? Storming such a mountain would require days of bombardment and several waves of storm troopers, not to mention all kinds of modern close combat equipment, including mortars and flamethrowers."

Maßmann watches the light blue smoke playing around his cigar.

"Annaberg! If we snatched that from the insurgents, we'd take away all faith in their cause. Annaberg is to the Catholic insurgents what Lourdes is to the devout French...."[66]

He snaps his fingers.

"It's a beautiful dream! But my artillery munitions have been lost near Ohlau."

An excited Bergerhoff paces up and down the room. "Damn good idea, Annaberg! A few more companies, and we'd overrun those Poles in a daring assault. Deliver some good tidings from the German Reich to those astonished monks and clerics who have already begun to sing their sermons for the good Lord across the border!"

Gogolin is enthusiastic.

"We'd control the whole upper Oder area!"

For a while, the stranger feasts on the confusion and surprise caused by his seemingly pointless suggestion. Then he offers a brief bow.

"I didn't come here as a storyteller, gentlemen. The first detachments have already arrived a few days ago; tomorrow the bulk of our Freikorps 'Oberland' will follow! And our men have no intention of getting used to the climate around here."

The Freikorps leaders whirl around to face him.

Oberland?

That changes things!

Naturally, the general remains skeptical.

"And what kind of a miracle corps is that supposed to be?"

The young Oberlander laughs.

"It is quite interesting that the opponents of folkish freedom appear to be better acquainted with our corps than what is commonly referred to as the 'national' circles in Germany. Ask the red groups who proclaimed their little soviet republic in Munich two years ago who Captain Östereicher is, and you will witness some rather spectacular temper tantrums. Östereicher is one of our most important men inside the corps. Ask for Kolm and

---

[66] Lourdes is a French city, popular as a destination for pilgrimages due to a series of Marian apparitions in the nineteenth century. Annaberg is a small mountain located above the town of Sankt Annaberg (Góra Świętej Anny in Polish) in Upper Silesia. Much like Lourdes in France, it is an important destination for Catholic pilgrims in Poland. It is known for its carved depiction of the Virgin and Child with Saint Anne.

Diebitsch, who have become famous as the liberators of Munich. Ask for the man who sent the red Hoffmann government packing during the Kapp days, and you will learn that it was a young lieutenant Östereicher, who also belongs to us. Ask those ultramontane spooks who are plaguing Munich these days; ask Mr. Kahr and all his particularists [67] about Freikorps Oberland, and they will tell you that they would be more than glad to see us die a hero's death."

"Took your time getting here...," murmurs the chief of staff.

"Some of our men have come all the way from Tyrol. If you have a look at the map I think you'll find that it is located to the south, quite a few miles away," the Oberlander states laconically.

Maßmann reaches out to shake his hand.

"A couple more of those miracles, and I solemnly swear to establish the German border at the Caucasus with you gentlemen, if necessary."

That is too much for the general.

"I urge you, gentlemen, not to juggle such inane ideas. Not even in jest."

"No, no," von Eicken soothes him, clearly enjoying the situation. "For the time being, we'll just head to Annaberg, then to Berlin, and when that's done we'll consider a few of the neighboring continents!"

The general drums his fingers against the table, clearly irritated by now.

"I don't want to hear you talking about Annaberg either, gentlemen."

The Freikorps leaders exchange some meaningful glances. An almost mischievous drawl is playing around Maßmann's lips.

"We will try to burden your conscience as little as possible, General."

The leaders are already about to leave, when the general gives them one final wave.

"Remember that any indiscipline contains the seeds of rebellion!"

---

[67] In this context, particularism refers to Bavarian separatist and related tendencies, i.e. an exaggerated focus on Bavarian affairs (as opposed to an overarching German perspective).

Chapter 20

The camp is in a merry uproar. Although Heenemann swears that the roebuck ran into his line of fire with suicidal intent, his lying skills are not enough to avoid a dressing-down by the lieutenant. Ultimately though, the damage caused really isn't all that bad, seeing how the prohibition period will be over in two weeks anyway. Plus, the camp diet isn't exactly known for causing the men to despise some culinary variation.

Besides, Heenemann is an expert when it comes to playing down his rather frequent hunting accidents with little references to his imminent death on the battlefield. It could happen any day now! And surely no one could find anything reprehensible about a modest last meal?

Only once did he get in actual trouble with Maßmann. The lieutenant had been furious when, on a Friday morning, Heenemann had returned with a large basket full of pike, carp and perch, meekly admitting during the subsequent interrogation that he had acquired these tasty fish by means of hand grenades. Even his shy remark that in Catholic areas (Upper Silesia being no exception) it was customary to eat fish on Fridays was met with little understanding from his lieutenant.

Today's joy over Heenemann's hunting prowess is all the greater because the lieutenant, completely against his usual habits, has donated a large drum of beer.

The reason for this donation has remained unknown, but it is rumored that great events are in store for the volunteers.

Felix Teuscher has brought out his accordion and is playing tirelessly. And the soldiers never tire of singing all of their songs, from the first to the last verse.

For some reason these particular songs contain more tender thoughts of home than all the countless postcards and letters they have sent out over the last week.

Maßmann sits amidst his men.

Again they have asked him to sign his name among at least a hundred cards and letters, ideally with a few personal lines as well.

The lieutenant now knows their joys and sorrows, the desires and worries of his soldiers. To each of them he has talked about their home, about wives, children, and friends. He knows how to write down a few personal thoughts without too many words. The men are proud that their leader takes a personal interest in their private little worlds.

Sometimes Maßmann cannot help but think that it would be a pity not to collect and publish these men's letters.

That would be a proper lesson for those journalist hacks, who have never bothered to look into the hearts and minds of these Freikorps soldiers, abandoned by their state and homeland. And yet they have the audacity to paint them as brutalized Landsers—a danger to morality and justice! *If only they could read these letters,* thinks Maßmann, *perhaps then those venal scribblers would be just a little ashamed at the sight of the spiritual chastity permeating these simple sentences and questions.*

One only has to take a glimpse at a single sentence written by Riehl's brother-in-law in his letter home to feel the abundance of moral courage and heartfelt sentiments within it: "I think a lot about all of you and whether the children will become good Germans if I should end up falling on this battlefield…"

Sometimes Maßmann can feel his heart constrict with the happiness of getting to lead these men. Men who, despite their harsh fate condemning them to live alone, as outcasts, nevertheless found the strength to choose this life; to affirm their choice during the most bizarre of circumstances, and joyfully offer their comradeship to death himself.

He pulls a newspaper clipping out of his pocket, given to him by Martin Harke.

A well-known Berlin newspaper running a front-page notice announcing that contrary to popular rumors, there are no Freikorps in Upper Silesia, that the formation of such insane groups would be impossible anyway. That the government has threatened to punish any attempt at forming or participating in a Freikorps with three months in prison and a fine of up to one hundred thousand marks—all on the basis of the London

Ultimatum.[68]

Maßmann spits.

Whosoever loves his nation shall be made to pay a fine!

Whosoever dares to protect the heart of his people shall be imprisoned.

What a pathetic time! Don't the men who are cleaning their rifles over there, a happy tune on their lips, don't these men love the world? Don't they love their wives and their small children?

His gaze glides over to Louise, who is once again surrounded by a swarm of soldiers in need of her help. One has jammed his finger while cleaning his rifle, another one urgently needs a couple of buttons, the next one asks for her signature on a letter to his bride, and yet another one would love to have a book lent to him.

Louise knows how to get along with soldiers.

Her gentle hands know how to bandage small wounds caused by faulty cartridges and hand grenades, and her friendly words settle all kinds of disagreements and frictions.

And so they never dare to curse or utter harsh words in her presence. If one of the soldiers has a bride, he respects her in Louise; whoever has a mother shows reverence to Louise.

Right now she is reading a letter from Konrad Ertel's mother. Konrad has given it to her.

She reads it very quietly, so that only Konrad can hear it and doesn't have to worry about someone uninvited listening in and mocking him.

My dear boy!

Whenever I see your school friends on the street, it pierces my heart to know that you left school to become a soldier. You know how much I suffered in those days, when father was in the field, and every letter could have brought me that terrible message. And I fear for you even more than that, because you are still half a child, and there is no reporting whatsoever in the newspapers about that war you are waging in Silesia. Instead, there are all the more rumors of bloody battles.

Father becomes very serious when we talk about you in the evenings. I can tell that he tries to hide his worries about you from me. A few days ago he was asked to see the principal of your high school. The principal told him that a conference had ordered your dismissal because you are participating in an illegal

---

[68] A reference to the previously mentioned London conference that led to the occupation of several German cities in the Ruhr area.

organization. I believe this has led to a heated argument between your father and your former principal. His ears must have been ringing!

I don't want to make things more difficult for Father and so I often cry to myself at night. Just stay healthy, my boy, and try not to be too reckless. When you are back at home, we'll have all your favorite foods for a week. And I will get Father to give you that light motorcycle you have wanted for so long.

By the way, all of your classmates came to see me yesterday. They wanted to make it a protest visit against your dismissal. Of course, all of them envy you and wanted to hear exactly what you've been doing. Unfortunately, I know so very little myself. Your Lotte from dance class came over as well and asked me for a picture of yours. You should write to her.

I would love to send you a parcel, but the post office refuses to accept parcels addressed to your Freikorps.

Have you found nice comrades yet? So far we have only gotten three postcards, which only said your address and that you were doing well.

Please come back soon. I think of you day and night, my boy.

Your mother

Louise carefully replaces the letter in its envelope.

She can see that the ink has been smudged in a few places. She knows that Konrad's mother was in tears when she wrote this letter.

"Tonight I'll write a detailed letter to your mother, telling her exactly what you've already learned in our Freikorps and how much you are liked and respected by your comrades. And I'm sure the lieutenant will add a few words saying that he considers you a real man."

Konrad nods happily.

"I would be very grateful if you could do that. I'm not so good at writing what I really want to say in letters. And I'm also a little afraid of writing too gently. I'm not a child anymore, you know."

Louise would love to give this big boy a kiss on the forehead right now.

Chapter 21

Maßmann has scheduled a roll call for seven o'clock in the evening.

Today the Freikorps is supposed to receive their storm flag, in a grand ceremony. Louise has spent many hours huddled over the black cloth, embroidering the skull with silver threads.

Now the skull adorns one side of the flag, surrounded by a semicircle of letters:

O.S. 1921[69]

The other side announces:

THE BLACK GUARD

And yet another word below, like an order:

FREEDOM

Its stock was fashioned from oak by the local Schwesterwitz carpenter. Maßmann is pleased with the flag.

At five minutes to seven, the Freikorps is formed up in an open rectangle.

Sergeant Lemke salutes.

The lieutenant examines his corps. He can tell that there have been noticeable improvements in its soldierly bearing over the last few days. The men stand like trees under their steel helmets.

Heaven knows, it must be a tremendous feeling to lead such soldiers into battle!

There is a bright, hard sound to Maßmann's speech, as he tells them of

---

[69] O.S. is short for "Oberschlesien" (Upper Silesia). Various historic medals from the Upper Silesian Freikorps campaigns bear the same inscription.

the black corps under dukes Oels, Schill, and Lützow.[70]

"We shall prove ourselves worthy of this tradition. For our reward, we expect nothing less than what Schill found at Stralsund.[71] Remember, comrades, that from this day onward, death shall smile down on us from the very flag we carry into battle. Let it be a reminder to all of us, readily to accept that gravest of sacrifices. Never shall we waver in the face of despair. But let it also be a threat to our enemies, that we intend to deal death to anyone and anything that dares to oppose our march toward freedom."

Fuchsberger solemnly waves the flag as Maßmann raises his hand to his cap, hailing the eternal life of the German nation.

For the first time ever, the lieutenant reviews his marching corps.

Lemke leads the first company, Teuscher the second, Napoleon the third.

There is no marching band, nothing in the way of a lively rhythm. But the sheer force with which the men perform the parade more than makes up for it. To Maßmann, it merely adds to the gravity of it all.

He thinks of that day in Potsdam when his Folkish Wanderers carried the green flag, the flag of the prophet.

The corps celebrates until deep into the night.

Napoleon and Martin Harke are tirelessly inventing new jokes, and performing increasingly daring pranks without a care in the world.

The men are bursting with laughter as Napoleon transforms into a buxom peasant girl with the help of a brightly colored embroidered headscarf, a bright red flannel underskirt, and a white blouse. Even more so when, with a deep curtsy, he asks the lanky Harke to join him in a *Krakowiak*.[72]

Fuchsberger strains his accordion so much that one might think he was hell-bent on tearing it to pieces.

Heenemann, wearing a frock coat, secretly borrowed from the Twardawa sacristan, has disguised himself as a bourgeois parliamentarian. He delivers a raucous sermon against soldiers in general and the Black Guard volunteers in particular, carefully interspersed with lovely Reichstag

---

[70] Friedrich Wilhelm von Braunschweig-Oels, Ferdinand von Schill, and Ludwig Adolf Wilhelm von Lützow were Freikorps leaders during the Napoleonic Wars.
[71] Ferdinand von Schill died defending the town of Stralsund against the French in 1809.
[72] The *Krakowiak* is a fast Polish folk dance.

phrases. The chair breaking under his feet in the middle of the speech only adds to the hilarity of it all.

Chapter 22

Duty continues the next morning at six o'clock, as per usual. Maßmann attaches particular importance to his men's hand grenade drills.

Konrad Ertel is eager to learn and has proven to be particularly adept at throwing live hand grenades. Maßmann places him in the special assault squad, whose leadership he has entrusted to Harke.

With great pride and a little white oil paint, Konrad adds the small question mark to his steel helmet. The assault squad has chosen it as its special feature, to be added directly below the large skull and bones all Freikorps members wear on their steel helmets.

He is extremely grateful to his uncle Heenemann for making him a part of the Black Guard. And he's all the more pleased that his Freikorps in particular has managed to obtain good uniforms, making them into a cohesive unit. Some of the other formations are looking more like a bunch of brigands—purely from lack of suitable equipment.

Heenemann too is quite pleased to see that his nephew is developing into a good soldier, although he studiously avoids letting him see that satisfaction.

What really matters to him is how Konrad will carry himself in his first battle. That is why he is sparing in his praise. He considers inappropriate praise a danger to Konrad's developing character.

Seeing his agility and eagerness, the Freikorps has taken to calling the boy their hound.

Every morning Konrad longs to greet the sun, hoping that it will not set on this day without bringing about his baptism by fire.

At times a heart-clenching fear rises in him—what if the Freikorps would be kept in camp too long and then one day it would be too late? An armistice could be made, the corps disbanded without the flag ever having seen battle.

One day Maßmann took the hound aside and asked what exactly was bothering him so much.

Konrad told the lieutenant about his fears.

Laughing heartily, Maßmann just gave him a slap on the shoulder.

"Trust me boy, a real warrior is never late. And the war Germany has been forced into in 1914 will never truly end until justice prevails in this world. But that may take another fifty, perhaps even another hundred years, no matter the number of peace dictates in between. Because the world simply does not want to be just. Its ruling powers consider their arbitrary decisions to be more suitable for the preservation of their status quo."

Ever since then, Konrad has become much calmer, trusting that his lieutenant won't send him home without giving him an opportunity to perform great deeds.

But when the rattle of machine guns and the detonation of mines and grenades drone on in the east, he clutches his rifle tighter, eagerly wishing to be over there.

The population is friendly and supports the soldiers with everything that their modest means allow them to give.

There are only a few who harbor an irreconcilable hatred for the Germans: a hatred instilled in them by fanatical Catholic clergymen or emissaries of Korfanty, promising them heaven on earth once their detachment from the German Reich has been completed.

They have managed to convert a young teacher from the local neighborhood, who now uses his knowledge, painstakingly acquired at German schools and universities, to alienate parents and children from their German homeland.

The soldiers have long suspected the teacher of espionage. On more than one occasion they have observed him skulking around near the camp, asking peasants about all sorts of things concerning the Freikorps. So far, though, they were unable to prove conclusively that he was delivering intelligence to the enemy. And if one of the soldiers hurried to question the teacher, he could be certain that the latter would simply kneel down at one of the many crucifixes erected at crossroads and fields to immerse himself in sheer endless prayers.

Maßmann gives orders to saddle the sorrel which he had received from the stables of Count Oppersdorf a few days ago.

Bergerhoff had called earlier, asking Maßmann to come over for a meeting around mid-morning.

Near Twardawa, the sorrel suddenly becomes restless. Maßmann bends over the horse's neck, trying to soothe it with a few pats.

At that very moment, a shot rings out at close range. The sorrel mounts, whinnying and wailing, then tumbles to the ground.

Maßmann has the greatest difficulty avoiding being crushed by the falling animal. Out of the corner of his eyes, he can see the teacher jump up from behind a crucifix and run away.

The pistol shot has penetrated the sorrel's neck, tearing the artery.

Blood gushes out in violent bursts, as thick as a man's arm.

Taking out his own pistol, Maßmann puts down the horse and hurries back to camp.

It takes him just a few minutes to reach Bergerhoff on the phone and explain the situation.

"That wretch still has to be prowling around near your camp."

"I'll make every effort to track him down," Bergerhoff promises.

Three hours later, he calls again.

"We've caught him near Trawnig. I'll have him brought over to your camp!"

Now the teacher stands in front of Maßmann.

The insolence with which he used to confront German soldiers has completely left him.

It seems that his capture may not have been particularly gentle.

Pale and trembling, he looks at the man whom he had just tried to ambush and kill a few hours ago.

A last vestige of manhood prevents him from begging for mercy, sparing Maßmann the added disgust.

The protocol remains short.

With trembling fingers the teacher signs the document, dropping the pen twice.

"A good Catholic like yourself, how could you choose that hiding place for your attack? A crucifix, of all things?"

The other remains silent, scowling at the ground.

Maßmann beckons to Napoleon.

"You will transport this man to Oberglogau. Have them give you a receipt!"

Napoleon clicks his heels and salutes.

Half an hour later, their car rattles off with the prisoner.

Maßmann is astonished when Napoleon reports back after an inconceivably short time.

"What's wrong?"

Napoleon looks at him from clear eyes.

"Obediently reporting that I shot and buried the prisoner with my own hands in a little grove just outside Oberglogau."

Maßmann jumps up from his chair, shouting at him.

"Have you gone completely mad, man?"

Napoleon's attitude remains unchanged. His voice takes on an almost crystalline tone.

"What were they going to do with him in Oberglogau? A few weeks in jail at the very most. And then he would have been free to walk around the place again, with a little martyr's crown to boot."

"How on earth would you know? Couldn't they just as well have done a court martial at Oberglogau, lawfully sentencing him to death?"

Napoleon shakes his head with determination.

"They wouldn't have done that. Someone who hasn't even the courage to sign our attack orders will be all the more hesitant to pass a death sentence. Why bother plaguing the gentlemen in Oberglogau with a bad conscience? So I took the responsibility upon myself. Also, we didn't catch that teacher in open combat. In my eyes, and certainly in the eyes of any decent soldier, he did not act like a warrior, but like a pig. And pigs...."

He shrugs and breaks off.

Maßmann puts his hand on Napoleon's shoulder. It weighs heavy.

"I understand you. Now I am sorry that I did not execute his sentence myself. But the responsibility lies with me alone. Remember that."

Silently the men light a cigarette, musing after the smoke.

Napoleon's hands are trembling a little, causing ash to fall from his cigarette.

With an almost curious timidity, he occasionally glances at the index finger of his right hand. The finger that pulled the trigger!

Maßmann recognizes the struggle that stirs within the heart of his third company leader.

He knows that he has to make him speak now to get rid of the pressure that threatens to choke him.

"Did he die badly?"

Napoleon walks around the room with long strides. He makes a sudden stop in front of Maßmann, breathing heavily.

"He must have known that this was the end for him, because he just kept looking at me with those eyes. Kind of like you would imagine a death row inmate staring at his executioner as he climbs the penultimate rung of the ladder leading to the gallows. I could see the whites of his eyes shining in the twilight."

Suddenly Napoleon buries his face in his hands.

A convulsive twitching runs through his whole body.

Maßmann waits for his agitation to subside.

Slowly, Napoleon lowers his hands. His face has turned ashen.

"He asked me not to torture him and to see to it that he would not just lie there, unburied. I promised him that I would. When we reached the place, I gave him five minutes to collect himself, think about life and death. Before the five minutes were up, he nudged me and said he was ready; he wanted to die like a man. He didn't have any regrets, his world would be over if Germany ended up winning. Then he just placed his head against the muzzle of my pistol. I calmly pulled the trigger. He only reared up once more and was dead within seconds. I buried him under a birch tree. You'll always be able to find it, because the white birch shines far throughout the forest."

Heavily, he sinks into a chair, resting his head sideways on the table.

Maßmann turns off the light and quietly leaves the room.

In the morning, Maßmann and Louise visit the Krappitz hospital.

Its chief physician is kind and courteous.

"Of course we'll employ your wife. We have a shortage of trained forces. Wounded people are brought in every day, and we really weren't prepared for an actual war."

Louise is pale, restless.

Her eyes keep trying to catch Karl's gaze.

"Please just give me as much work as possible, Doctor!"

Maßmann strokes her trembling hand.

"Let's not hope for too much work."

Then he bows to the chief physician.

"I know my wife will be in good hands with you. And I hope she will be useful here, especially over the next few days."

The doctor pricks up his ears

"Are you planning a special operation?"

Maßmann steps toward the window, looking in the direction of Annaberg.

"The next few days will see heavy fighting and much blood."

His voice has gone quiet.

"I fear...." With a wave of his hand, he breaks off.

The doctor notices that Louise is looking for something to hold on to.

He discreetly pushes a chair toward her. Louise bites her lips and closes her eyes. *If only he doesn't notice!*—she forces herself to focus on this thought, again and again. He mustn't know her secret!

The doctor is now standing next to Maßmann, at the window.

He knows that in situations like these, a coarse word is more valuable than dozens of pleasantries.

"Don't even think of coming back here as a patient though. We don't do private nurses."

Maßmann gives him a grateful look.

Gently, he places a hand on the crown of his wife's hair. "I'll be back very soon, Louise. Be brave. Always remember that a soldier's wife can be the proudest of all women, for she must also bear the greatest suffering."

Louise nods.

Again and again she nods. Only when the door closes and Karl's footsteps have started to fade away does she starts sobbing. Then she hurries to the window for one more glance at Karl.

Chapter 23

At Oberglogau, the orderlies are running around like headless chickens. The telephones are buzzing incessantly. An excited fever has gripped the men, even causing the general to rumble off every now and then.

The Freikorps officers have begun to strike notes that have become virtually indistinguishable from open mutiny.

Bergerhoff roars loud enough to make the thick veins on his forehead bulge:

"Damn it all to hell, what on earth are we here for, anyway? Do you perhaps want us to raise a white flag and defect? If we stay in camp, we'll be overrun before three days have passed!"

"Yes," Eicken agrees, "Bergerhoff is absolutely right. Every single day the insurgents have received fresh reinforcements. Today there are already fifteen enemies for every soldier of ours. In a few days there will be twenty, perhaps even twenty-five. All indicators point to a new offensive that will begin between May 23rd and May 25th. We have to attack now, if only for the sake of simple self-preservation."

The general is furious.

"You are being mad, gentlemen. Just yesterday I obtained government permission for us to shift toward a more mobile defensive strategy. I'll be in hot water if you start recklessly pursuing your own agenda."

The chief of staff tries to calm things down.

"If you gentlemen just make some slight advances, you'll worry the enemy enough to tie him to his positions. In my opinion, that would be more than enough."

Maßmann shakes his head.

"Not only are half-measures exceedingly stupid, experience shows that they are also dangerous. In order to be able to wage a successful defensive struggle, not even mentioning the notion of trench warfare, we would need many times our current manpower and armaments. Just imagine if we were to return to our initial positions after a small advance and the enemy was to follow! Don't you know what that would mean for us?"

The chief of staff weighs his head thoughtfully.

Obviously he is finding it rather difficult to speak out against his real convictions.

"Well, tactics has always been the art of using the available resources to assure success while avoiding risks as much as possible. According to this definition, you are rather poor tacticians, gentlemen, seeing how you strive for uncertain success using inadequate means."

"We don't give a damn about tactics." A more than dry response by the Oberlander. "Clearly you are entirely unfamiliar with higher strategic concepts; otherwise this plan of ours would not be quite so astonishing to you."

He gives the stunned general a short bow and an ironic smile.

"Perhaps the youth has something that is superior to even the best and most proven of all strategic systems. I am talking about faith, General. True, it might not be the faith to move mountains. But it is the one to storm them."

"Faith, faith." The words are visibly tearing at the general. "What does that word even mean these days? When our reality is being formed by nothing but brute force and numerical superiority?"

With a sober look, he turns to the Oberlander.

"At this moment I consider any discussion of strategy and tactics to be more than superfluous. Not even to mention faith." Slowly he rises, his hand resting heavily on the table. "I deeply regret not being able to listen to your rather far-fetched objections any longer, gentlemen. I hereby forbid you to take any independent action in combating the enemy. That is an order. And I will see to it that my orders are obeyed."

As Maßmann watches the Freikorps leaders, he can see anger and disappointment on every single face.

Bringing about a complete break with the general does not seem advisable to him at this time.

He gestures to the Oberlander, who is about to launch into an angry protest.

"We understand you quite well, General. You are worried that things might happen too fast, causing you to lose control of the situation. In the same vein, I am sure you also understand our concern that inaction might damn us to become a plaything at the whims of our enemies. After all, it is the very nature of the Freikorps not only to compensate for deficiencies in equipment through superior mobility, but most importantly, to thwart our enemies' ability to engage in any kind of long-term planning."

"We'll have time enough for partisan fighting after we have been crushed. But I'd like to see someone try that first," Bergerhoff growls toward the general.

The chief of staff gives an appeasing smile.

"That's only a last resort. Let's not think of that today."

"Will you finally allow us to prove our worth, here? You have my word that my men and I will willingly obey your tactics if the Freikorps approach should fail. But until that happens, I will remain steadfast and stubborn."

Von Eicken smirks, rubbing his hands together.

Gogolin crushes his cigar butt and winks at the Freikorps leaders.

"I can't quite shake this odd feeling of embarrassment. It feels as if we've been going round and round in circles. For days now."

"Quite true," the general responds, "It seems like you still haven't quite made up your mind as to whether you should obey or mutiny."

"Mutiny is a bit much," interjects von Eicken. "After all, we never put ourselves under your command."

"But gentlemen…" the chief of staff wants to mediate, but is interrupted by Maßmann.

"We have no intention whatsoever of tearing up our already quite-sparse front. On the contrary, we want to establish as united a front as humanly possible. It is regrettable that our opinions as to the required measures differ so significantly. However, considering that the Freikorps form the liveliest nucleus of the entire German resistance, we can hardly be expected to relinquish our life force, General. And that life force is total mobility. I believe it would be best if we didn't try to cause any unnecessary trouble for each other."

The general shakes his head disapprovingly.

"The difficulties are entirely on your side, gentlemen."

Gogolin jumps up from his chair.

"You can blame me or not, I don't care. I've had enough of this. Our men are dying outside and we can't agree on whether to stall or strike. I'm off to strike now. Goodbye, General."

The Freikorps leaders cheer at his words.

"We meet tonight in Twardawa," Maßmann nods to his comrades, before looking the general in the eye. "I will not give my men the impression that you are our enemy, General. On the contrary, I will even take the liberty of extending your warmest greetings to them."

"Please do so," the general readily agrees, "You can believe me that I am your and your soldiers' best friend. Don't confuse me with a pacifist or a Social Democrat, but you need to understand that I possess the government's confidence, which I have no intention of abusing."

"You will have no reason to be ashamed of us," Maßmann continues, after receiving the general's words with an obliging bow, "Your objections to our intentions have been noted. You consider our plan to attack the enemy by surprise to be nonsensical and infeasible. Any future actions of ours will be outside of your responsibility. I confirm that you are in no way responsible for any of the events to come. Please have this put in writing."

The general's hand trembles.

He can see that these men have rejected his influence and that he has been excluded from their meeting with destiny at Annaberg.

His voice has lost its timbre and turned brittle.

"I could accuse you of mutiny, even though you may feel justified in refusing this accusation. I could attempt to bind you to my command by word of honor. I care just as much about our fatherland as you do, gentlemen, and I cannot believe that you would deny me the sincerity of my honor and personal convictions. I am an old soldier. It pains me to see these barriers of misunderstanding erected between us, that you may secretly decry me as indecisive, perhaps even cowardly. I am much older than most of you, by decades. That may be a disadvantage. However, my many years as a soldier have taught me that the only true bond, the only true obligation, is a man's word. And I have given my word to the government, as its trustee. I would have to turn this pistol against myself for supporting your scheme."

The general's words are followed by a long silence.

The young officers can sense the struggle taking place in the old man's soul. They cannot help but respect the fate of this irreproachable knight of a bygone era, a time when only men of honor were allowed to accept a word of honor. A question crosses Maßmann's mind: *should we tell the old man that he wasted his word on scoundrels?* But it seems better not to mention it. The other officers urge him to leave.

Maßmann squeezes the general's hand.

"We have realized that in this world of ours, only instinct is valid. It makes us wary of all snares and traps set by weaklings. Yet it leads us to even more vigorous affirmation and appreciation of true strength."

An orderly enters for a report to the general.

The general winces in response.

"The Berlin commissar has arrived? In person? Have him come in."

The officers prick up their ears, once again approaching the general.

The latter nods gravely.

"Please stay for another moment, gentlemen, so you can convince yourself of the love Berlin has for you and your ideas."

A few moments later, the commissar enters the room, greeting the general with amiable nonchalance.

Maßmann cannot suppress a smile.

God knows, it is the same commissar who was so eager to ruin his life in Berlin.

The general points to the officers.

"I have just had a discussion with these gentlemen, Commissar. It appears that there have been some misunderstandings regarding the official government position, so I believe it would be appropriate if you could provide them with some explanations."

"Gladly," the commissar hastens, "I welcome the opportunity."

The officers begin to grumble.

Bergerhoff cannot refrain from muttering something that sounds a lot like "slime-ball."

The commissar shoots him a sideways glance and receives a cheerful grin in return.

Then he examines the Freikorps leaders, one after another.

When he spots Maßmann, he offers a brief bow.

"I knew I would find you here, Lieutenant."

"I admire your shrewdness, Commissar! Where else would I be but here at the front?"

The commissar shows no sign of the annoyance he feels at this rebuke.

"I am in the enviable position of being able to inform you that the negotiations which the government has been engaging in with the greatest vigor for the past weeks have at last produced the desired result. The Inter-Allied Commission is ready to bring about a truce between the fighting parties."

"Oh, that's just great," Bergerhoff interjects. "I'm sure the insurgents will be kind enough to just gather up their weapons and go home."

"Please refrain from interrupting me with such derisive comments," the commissar defends himself, turning to the general. "These Freikorps leaders seem to be leading a rather carefree life here."

The general offers a surly smile.

At the bottom of his soldier's heart, this slick commissar from Berlin is nothing but loathsome to him.

"You know that my command only extends as far as the self-defense battalions, Commissar. Freikorps are Freikorps; they don't just listen to your every word."

The commissar swallows this pill as well.

"Of course the planned ceasefire can only happen on a status quo basis, meaning that both parties will retain their positions. A neutral zone is to be created between the combatants."

"So that means we will have to acknowledge their invasion and sanction all of the territorial gains they made so far," Maßmann states matter-of-factly.

"You don't negotiate with burglars, you shoot to kill, unless you want to be shot down yourself first," von Eicken thunders.

"Do you think we came here as bankruptcy lawyers?" sneers the Oberlander.

Gogolin waves his hand in a contemptuous gesture.

"Berlin seems to have fallen prey to some pretty adorable optimism."

The commissar clears his throat, visibly angry now.

"I don't expect you to be able to judge the overall political situation, gentlemen; it is far too complicated."

"You don't say," the Oberlander smiles. "For us down here the situation is looking as clear as day."

The commissar raises his voice.

"I refuse to discuss processes and events which you are simply unable to understand. Three days from now, the English will insert their troops between the current positions. Afterwards, all you have to do is await further orders from Berlin."

Bergerhoff steps up to the commissar and grabs him by the button of his cutaway.

"You can tell your highly esteemed government in Berlin they can… we will forward our instructions to them in due time!"

The commissar tears himself away from him. "General, I ask for your protection."

The general glances at his chief of staff. "You will have to excuse me, Commissar, urgent official business...."

With that, he walks toward the door, accompanied by the chief of staff.

The commissar is stunned.

"Surely you don't want to hand me over to these Freikorps leaders, General?"

The general turns around once more.

"Your discussions with these gentlemen are none of my business, Commissar. I'll be back in an hour or so. Then I'll be at your full disposal."

No sooner has the door slammed behind the two men than Bergerhoff gives Gogolin a nudge in the ribs.

"Very decent of the old man!"

The commissar nervously paces up and down the room, haunted by the looks of the Freikorps leaders.

"You have to understand my position here. Please believe me that it is not easy for me to stand before you as an adversary."

"No one is forcing you to do that," von Eicken remarks.

The commissar's voice takes on an almost pleading tone.

"Be reasonable, gentlemen! It is better for Germany to temporarily lose a few square miles than to risk an open conflict and cause much greater damage in the process. The government has the greatest respect for your courage and sense of duty. But we ask you to trust its superior political foresight."

"That is precisely what we are looking to avoid at all cost," interrupts the Oberlander.

The commissar regains some of his former composure.

"I would like to call your attention to the fact that I have the power to negotiate amicably with you gentlemen. If, however, you decide to cause fundamental difficulties, I have also brought certain orders with me. Namely, orders to dissolve your Freikorps."

The Oberlander slaps his knee with laughter.

"Oh, that was a splendid little speech you gave there, Commissar, quite splendid."

"You seem to forget that I have the authority to proceed against you by any means necessary."

"Nobody is going to deny your authority to do so," Maßmann states with a smile, "Yet there is also the question of whence you will get the power to act on that authority."

"You dare to mutiny against official government orders?" the commissar asks sharply. "Are you aware that by doing so, all of you will incur charges of high treason?"

"One may argue about such terms," the Oberlander replies, entirely calm. "But in any case it is still better to commit treason against a government than to be a traitor to one's country. And there can be no bigger traitors to our country than those who negotiate instead of acting in times of danger."

The Freikorps leaders signal their approval. There is no need for further discussion.

The commissar can see that it is entirely useless to further expose himself to the men's attacks.

"I have come to the conclusion that you are incorrigible. In the name of the government, I hereby order the immediate disbanding of your corps. You will see to the immediate repatriation of your soldiers. Demonstrate your good intentions by carrying out these orders right away and I may be able to offer you an amnesty, although on an entirely optional basis."

Bergerhoff is about to hurl himself at the commissar and plant a couple of fists between his eyes.

Maßmann holds him back.

"Commissar, I believe we can all agree here that your government's orders are not particularly relevant to us. You know this. And so it shouldn't be too surprising to you that we intend to storm against the enemy one of these days. Conditions at the front, which I do not intend to discuss with you here, leave us no other choice."

The commissar slaps his palm on the table.

"You are going too far! I will ask the English to deploy their soldiers this very day."

"You won't be able to!"

The commissar pauses.

"What do you mean? Why not?"

Maßmann's voice is as calm as if he was discussing the weather. "Because you are my prisoner, Commissar!"

The latter is staggered.

"You have no right to do that!"

"But I do have the power!"

At a wave from Maßmann, the Freikorps leaders leave the room.

The commissar stands at the window. His face is yellow, like wax.

"You will be imprisoned for this!"

Maßmann laughs with disdain.

"Executions are quite rare among simpletons. They would have to catch you first."

The commissar's composure is gone.

His voice turns into a screech.

"Then run toward your doom, you idiots! We have already made sure that you won't get any ammunition, not a single bullet. You will be wiped off the face of the Earth! And those who the insurgents fail to mow down, we will catch at the border! You can count on that! Then we'll finally have peace! At last, the poor, miserable population will get to breathe a sigh of relief!"

Maßmann spits out in front of him.

"Swine!"

Then he pushes him back from the window.

Below the window, Napoleon and Fuchsberger are standing next to the car.

Napoleon's fist is clutching a hand grenade.

"Want me to come up?"

Maßmann waves him off.

Then he puts a hand on the commissar's shoulder.

"Let's go!"

As the car drives off, the general and his chief of staff observe them from one of the castle's balconies.

"I sure hope they don't kill that guy."

The chief of staff weighs his head serenely.

"Oh, he deserves it. Just as much as those who sent him here!"

Chapter 24

The camp is close to a riot when the car arrives with its prisoner. Heenemann in particular seems extremely eager to hit the commissar over the head with the butt of his rifle. "I have a score to settle with that lout!"

The look Maßmann gives him is enough to make Heenemann lower the rifle and step aside in shame.

Napoleon holds his sides with laughter.

God knows, the commissar is not exactly a heroic sight.

In Berlin, he was a master of penetrating looks, but out here, his eyes barely get off the ground!

His voice, pulling all the stops in Berlin, has become toneless.

Konrad has uncle Heenemann explain this mysterious prisoner to him. He can hardly believe that there could be such a thing as a German backstabbing other German fighters. Heenemann dismissively points his thumb toward the commissar, who is still standing somewhere behind them, surrounded by a large group of soldiers.

"You still need to learn what this world is like, my boy. There might be a whole lot of menfolk around, but there are darned few men on this Earth. The menfolk throw themselves at anyone who offers them opportunities for what they like to call 'advancement.' The menfolk do not have their own opinion; they always believe exactly what their bread-giver, what their superior believes. And if he should be replaced by someone else, the menfolk immediately switch to believing whatever the successor believes. They like to call this 'realism.' Just look at the commissar! He might have been quite a decent fella at some point. Swore an oath to Kaiser Wilhelm and kept it, always loyal and faithful. Until Fritz Ebert came along. And now he is just as loyal and faithful in his oath to Fritz Ebert. Regardless of what his conscience may be calling out to him, he does his so-called duty, which mainly consists of him coming here to try and dissolve us. And if we were to be at the helm tomorrow, he would swear loyalty and faith to our cause in a heartbeat, fight our enemies, and so on. He'd probably be quite good at it, too."

Konrad shakes his head in disbelief.

"What's in it for him? Where's the benefit in being such a wimp?"

"Oh," says Heenemann, pondering the question, "There simply are some people who have this comfortable tendency of always staying one hundred percent safe and secure, avoiding all decisions that might make life even a little uncomfortable. Somehow, they always get fed. Usually they even manage to get a decent pension, unless the rotten state they have helped to build up through their sycophancy goes bankrupt before they kick the bucket. Then the joke's on them. If that happens, they might even turn revolutionary and cry out for a new state that will guarantee them the pensions they so love. After all, they are loyal supporters of any well-off state."

Konrad shakes himself with disgust.

"I'd rather die like a dog than accept even a single penny from a state I detest."

Heenemann administers a paternal hair-ruffling.

"Well, that goes without saying, Konrad. And that's also why I brought you here, so you can learn what it means to be a man. Men don't sell themselves. But when it comes down to it, they don't seem to mind giving away their whole beautiful life. For free. And even for some things others may think entirely unimportant."

Having arrived in Maßmann's room, the commissar becomes downright trusting when he realizes that no one is threatening to harm him.

Maßmann has given him a short lecture on the Freikorps view of the situation in Upper Silesia as well as the necessary countermeasures that have to be taken.

"I realize that your views are quite justified, Lieutenant. People in Berlin do not realize just how serious the situation is at the moment."

Maßmann nods.

"My only reason for detaining you is so that you will be able to educate those very people once you return to Berlin."

The commissar's eyes light up with expectation.

"May I take your words to mean that I will be allowed to return to Berlin?"

"Before that, I would like to give you the opportunity to convince yourself of the realities of our struggle up to this point: a short visit to the battlefield."

The commissar is squirming.

"You're not seriously planning to drag me to the front, are you?"

Maßmann calls an orderly.

"Have Fuchsberger, Heenemann, and Teuscher drive up in the car!"

Their drive takes them to Körnitz, Krappitz and Gogolin.

The roads are guarded by members of the self-defense battalions. Their armaments are exceptionally poor. Only every third or fourth man has a rifle. There are no machine guns. Not a single one of them is wearing a uniform.

The commissar is visibly embarrassed.

Maßmann calls his attention to every single one of the little obstacles that German workers and peasants have erected from wagons, stones, boards, and bags of earth all along the roads.

"Here you can see that the German population is trying to fight, using every means at its disposal. The fact that their means are wholly insufficient is the fault of your government, Commissar. Or do you seriously believe that these well-intentioned, but ultimately useless precautions would allow them to resist a determined attack by the insurgents?"

The commissar silently shakes his head.

"Then you will finally be able to understand why the Upper Silesian Freikorps must not be disarmed. Whoever disarms the Freikorps destroys the very backbone of German resistance."

"I'm willing to do everything you want me to do; I could even try to get some of your arms transports released, Lieutenant!"

Maßmann gives him a meaningful glance.

"Even if you were being honest—it's too late to make amends for your government's crimes now."

Gogolin greets their car with a joyful roar.

He completely ignores the commissar, not even dignifying him with a single glance.

"I would like to show the gentleman from Berlin the mutilated men you found at the train station," Maßmann says, heartily shaking Gogolin's hand.

"Gladly! The English sent a commission yesterday, which recorded everything and confirmed its truth. After all, our gentlemen in Berlin prefer the English verdict over our mere German reports!"

Eleven German soldiers have been laid out in a shed.

Even Maßmann cannot bear the sight, so gruesome is the view of their mutilated corpses.

One is missing his eyes, another has had the top of his skull smashed in; a third body is literally riddled with bayonet wounds.

There is not a single one among them who could be said to have found his death by an honest bullet.

"Horrible, just horrible," stammers the commissar.

Gogolin reaches into his wallet and extracts a few pictures from it.

"These pictures were taken by the English. Maybe Berlin will be interested in them."

"Thank you," whispers the commissar, "I will present them to my superiors."

They proceed to the camp's fortifications. The haste with which they have been dug into the mountain slopes is obvious.

The commissar cannot help but gawk at them.

"But those are trenches, just like in the war."

Gogolin just offers a grim laugh.

A moment later, the commissar throws himself to the ground as a grenade howls past them.

"Oh, just get up, will you?" Fuchsberger laughs. "I'm sure the insurgents won't try to hurt you. Why would they go around attacking their best friends, after all?"

Gogolin has set up a twin telescope, allowing the commissar to observe the insurgents' front.

"What do you see up there?"

"Several trenches and machine gun nests, one on top of the other."

"Our men will have to storm these the day after tomorrow. Without a single shot of artillery support. Might even wake you up, Commissar! What do you see over there, to the right?"

Straining his eyes, the commissar searches.

"Those could be enemy artillery guns."

"Correct! They have set up four batteries over there. And they will use those to shoot down our men in their assault squads, which are already quite sparse. You think you got some room in your luggage to take the curses of those dying men with you, Commissar?"

This goes on for over half an hour.

The commissar cannot remember ever having experienced such mental torture.

"Isn't there anything I can do to help you?"

"If you actually report the truth of what you have seen here in Berlin, you will have done enough for us," Maßmann responds, his voice harsh.

The return trip takes them through a number of Freikorps camps.

All the men are practicing with great zeal.

Maßmann is content to wordlessly point out the thoroughly soldierly image of their small squads to the Commissar.

A deep blush has risen to the unfortunate man's face. His shame is palpable.

Chapter 25

The Freikorps leadership meeting at Twardawa lasts less than an hour.

Freikorps Oberland claims the honor of advancing into the Annaberg terrain for a reconnaissance mission in the early afternoon hours of May 20th, thus laying the groundwork for an attack.

Each of the men is aware of just how dangerous an enterprise it is. They must not fail, for their failure would mean an irreparable slump in the spirit of the German resistance.

The Freikorps leaders know that bearing defeats is an inevitable part of warfare.

But a defeat on the basis of flawed preparation is simply inexcusable!

That is why it is of the utmost importance that the Oberland reconnaissance mission succeeds, thus allowing them to determine the starting positions of the other Freikorps.

The Oberland officers' eyes are shining. They get to be the first to engage the enemy!

Their preliminary discussions over the last two days have determined a high-level plan of attack. With everyone in attendance, the plan is read out once again.

"The Black Guard will unite with the Chappuis attack column, made up of the Bergerhoff, Lensch, and Winkler battalions, in an attack on the enemy to the southwest of the Gogolin-Kandrzin railroad line. The Watzdorf battalion remains in reserve.

"The attack column Horadam,[73] made up of Freikorps Oberland and

---

[73] Ernst Horadam (1883–1956) was a World War I veteran and commander of Freikorps Oberland. He led and directed the storm on Annaberg.

battalion Heinz will advance toward the north and northeast.

"The Graf Strachwitz detachment will secure our left flank against the Groß-Steiner forest and intensify the attack on Groß-Stein."

They have scheduled the start of the assault for the early morning of May 21st, at half past two.

Von Eicken's assault company joins the undertaking, even though von Eicken's men in particular have been continuously occupied in the trenches from the first day of the insurgent invasion and have already taken considerable losses!

They proudly call themselves battalions, those seven weak detachments that want to storm against an enemy who is so profoundly superior in every regard.

Assault battalions without even the armaments of a regular company in conventional warfare!

Bergerhoff turns to Maßmann.

"Whatever will your splendid commissar report about us in Berlin?"

"When I dismissed him last night, he was almost falling over himself with good will. But I suspect his train ride back home will have gradually reverted him to a faithful servant of his treacherous state."

Gogolin is clearly harboring a grudge against the commissar.

"We should at least have given him a good thrashing, as a parting gift."

"We have other people to beat up now," shouts one of the Oberland officers, "Let's just leave those moral corpses to their spiritual decay!"

"I quite agree," nods Maßmann, "In front of us lies Annaberg. Leave everything behind us to vanish into fog."

Bergerhoff squeezes his hand.

"Goodbye, comrades!"

One by one, Maßmann walks up to his fellow officers, looking them firmly in the eyes and shaking their right hand.

"Long live our freedom. Long live our rebellion!"

Chapter 26

The marching orders cause great cheering in the camp. Konrad has tears in his eyes.

"Thank God we're not too late!"

Heenemann gives him a good-natured slap on the shoulder.

"Just you wait, my boy, until the bullets start whistling. Won't be cheering then. You're not a soldier until you've gotten over that fear."

Konrad turns away, huffing and puffing.

"Do you think I'm a coward?"

"Little chick," is all Heenemann says.

Lemke, Teuscher, and Napoleon present their companies.

A few days of good old Prussian drilling have worked wonders.

The men's grips snap into place, just like a guard regiment on parade. Rifles line up dead straight against their shoulders.

Not a muscle stirs in the men's faces.

Only the black skull and bones flag flutters heavily in the breeze.

Fuchsberger clenches its heavy oak stock in his fists.

A brief salute by Maßmann. He thanks the men for the report, allows himself a proud glance at his soldiers, then gives the command to march.

Nailed boots hit the bumpy pavement.

Maßmann marches at the head of his Freikorps.

Three yards behind him follows Fuchsberger with the flag. Another five yards and there marches Lemke, leader of the first company.

The hot sun burns down relentlessly from the sky. White dust rises from the road in dense, impenetrable clouds, settling like a veil on helmets, rifles and uniforms.

Martin Harke begins to sing.

His bright voice flutters across the corps, forcing the men to join in.

They sing the song they brought with them from the Baltic, hurling a soldier's proud defiance in the face of a world rife with cowards.

Ein Freikorps zog ins Baltikum,
Achthundert deutsche Soldaten.
So mancher wurde bleich und stumm,
Die Heimat hat ihn verraten.

One Freikorps walked the Baltic trail.
Eight hundred German soldiers strong.
More than one turned mute and pale,
Their country betrayed them all along.

In Riga floß viel deutsches Blut,
Die Düna färbte sich tiefrot.
Der alte deutsche Kämpfermut
Brach über Nacht des Landes Not.

At Riga German blood was shed,
The Duna red, the town in smoke.
Trusty German guts and lead
Freed this country from its yoke.

Die Fahne flattert hoch im Wind,
Zerschossen im Baltenlande.
Und alle, die gefallen sind,
Die fühlen nicht mehr die Schande.

Our flag is carried through the sky
Shot and scorched by Baltic flame.
And all of those who had to die,
No longer feel the shame.

Die Heimat hat sich von uns gewandt,
Als wir die Wunden ertrugen,
Hat unsres Kampfes Sinn verkannt,
Als wir unsre Schlachten schlugen.

The homeland has disowned our bands,
While we were marked with scars,
Spat on our sacrifice in these lands,
While we bravely fought their wars.

Wir zogen in den Kampf hinaus
Und wollten einst Könige sein.
Als Bettler kehren wir nach Haus.
Doch unsre Fahne, die blieb rein.

We went out to this bloody fight
Fame and glory on our mind,
As beggars we return tonight,
Our flag the purest of its kind.

The village girls run toward the road to wave at the sun-tanned men, rigorously marching off into danger, singing unconcernedly all the while.

Quite a few of the girls have tears in their eyes. Most likely they are thinking of a loved one who has been lying under fire at Gogolin or Krappitz for weeks.

Here and there a window is angrily slammed shut as the soldiers march by. This must be where the informers live: fanatical Catholics carrying on anti-German propaganda actions under the protection of their priestly garments.

In the afternoon above Körnitz, Maßmann allows the Freikorps some rest. The men are boisterous, just like schoolboys at the beginning of their summer holidays.

The waters of the Hotzenplotz are dark green and transparent all the way to the bottom. They get deeper and deeper until the small river finally joins the Oder.

Dusty uniforms are thrown off; the first men are already frolicking in the floods.

With a comfortable grin, Konrad stretches his limbs in the deep grass of the meadow. The farmers around here probably stopped mowing it for fear of stray bullets.

Dragonflies and butterflies are buzzing around. The sun conjures up trembling shadows playing under blades of grass swayed by the wind.

Bluish clouds steadily wander into an unknown distance, leaving home and enemy territory behind.

Konrad thinks of his boyhood dreams, which he once sent toward the wandering clouds. How long ago was that, anyway?

He wanted to become a circumnavigator in those days, explorer of unknown territories, an adventurer all over the world.

Those dreams have vanished, he thinks. But the reality of being a soldier is so much more beautiful than a dream ever could be.

Lost in thoughts, he chews the moisture from a long blade of grass.

What will it be like when the shells detonate around them?

Will it hurt a lot when you get hit by a bullet?

The comrades who have been in the war all say it's not really that bad, it just burns.

He startles. A wet clod of earth has hit his chest.

Heenemann laughs. "Scaredy-cat!"

Somewhat annoyed, Konrad gets up. He's feeling hungry. With long strides, he stalks across the meadow, toward a nearby farmhouse.

The farm looks deserted. The farmer is probably somewhere on his fields. Strange that there aren't any chickens on this farm. Did the farmer lock them up? Perhaps he is worried about inadvertently leading the soldiers into temptation.

An old watchdog blinks at him, lazily lying in his hut.

Konrad calls out to the farmhouse.

Finally, a young girl pokes her head from the stable door. *Pretty girl*, Konrad thinks, calling out a greeting to her. The girl smiles and comes closer. Well? What does he want?

The girl is maybe seventeen or eighteen years old. A colorful headscarf accentuates her fresh, healthy face. Her short skirt gives way to dainty calves.

She really is very pretty. Konrad's mind is stuck.

"Hey, you! What are you thinking about?"

It strikes Konrad that the girl's language sounds quite harsh.

"Can I get something to eat?"

The girl thinks for a moment, then nods.

"I can give you a piece of bread and a cup of milk. That's it. My parents went to Oberglogau this morning, and I don't know if they'd want me to give you any more."

Konrad follows the girl into the kitchen.

It is so cozy and clean in here. God knows, he hasn't been in a kitchen for a long time!

He awkwardly takes off his steel helmet and puts it on the table.

The girl cuts a thick slice of dark rye bread and puts a piece of bacon on it.

"Enjoy!"

The milk is cool and refreshing. Konrad drinks two large cups.

The girl has sat down next to him on the bench. She is quite pleased to see the young soldier's appetite.

"Are you going to attack?"

Konrad nods proudly.

"And you're not afraid?"

Konrad shakes his head in disdain.

"Afraid of the insurgents? No way!"

The girl sighs softly.

"They are cruel. Both of my brothers are at Gogolin. Two weeks ago they brought a neighbor's son home for his burial."

"We'll throw the insurgents back across the border," Konrad says with resolve.

The girl eyes him insistently.

"You're so young. And your hands are still so soft. You've never worked before, have you?"

Hesitantly and somewhat unwillingly, Konrad allows himself to be questioned and reports on what his life was like a short while ago, about his parents, his school, and his friends.

"Do you already have a bride?"

Konrad laughs. "Oh, there's still plenty of time for that!"

Then he gets up. "How much for the milk and bread?"

The girl acts offended.

Konrad offers his hand to her.

"Thank you very much! And goodbye!"

Suddenly the girl wraps her arms around his neck and kisses the boy on the mouth.

"Just come back!"

Konrad is taken aback. Silently he takes his steel helmet and leaves.

The girl follows him. Outside, she breaks off a budding twig from one of the lilac trees growing against the wall of the farmhouse.

"Yes, come back!"

He hastily puts the twig behind his belt and, without looking back again, walks over to his comrades.

Toward evening the Freikorps marches into Pietna.

The whole village has gathered to welcome the soldiers, who are busy assembling their rifles next to an old barn.

Boys and girls carry over refreshments: beer and milk, bread and sausages.

Maßmann has given orders that the rifles are not to be left unattended.

Incessant machine gun fire can be heard from the front. Between the salvos, there are the muffled bangs of shell impacts and exploding mines.

They are informed that Oberland's reconnaissance mission has been a complete success.

Fuchsberger has placed the unfurled black flag on two rifle pyramids so that the cloth just barely touches the ground.

He does not leave its side, never taking his eyes off the flag.

Lemke distributes a final round of mail. Most of it didn't get through to the front.

And so Heenemann is all the happier to see a letter from Marjelly. It contains a brand new picture of Ulrich. The boy has already grown so big! Heenemann can't get enough of it. Such large eyes on that little boy! On the back, Marjelly has added a greeting in mock child handwriting: "To my dear daddy!"

Everyone nearby has to take a look at the picture and examine it. Martin Harke, Teuscher, Lemke, Napoleon. All are full of praise. In the end, the picture is all smudged by rough warrior hands. Heenemann reverently rubs it clean with his handkerchief before carefully placing it in his breast pocket. Just above the heart.

Maßmann walks through the ranks of his men. "Make sure to write a letter home before we go into battle. And put a note with a home address in your pocket! Just in case."

Napoleon has the village youth gather a large pile of wood and lights it.

Silently, the men of the Black Guard write their farewells to the homeland.

Thoughtfully they scribble down their note and pocket it.

Konrad has had a boy fetch him a postcard. It depicts the usual panorama. Above the church there's a brown print: "Greetings from Pietna (Upper Silesia)."

Konrad doesn't quite know what to write.

Finally he takes up the pencil.

Dear Mother!

In a few hours our storm on Annaberg will begin. I am happy to be a part of it. Goodbye!

Your Konrad!

As he affixes the stamp, he looks closely at its inscription: *Haute Silesie.*

That's right! In a way, Upper Silesia is a foreign country now! Surely, one day this stamp will have the same value some of the old war stamps already have today. Like the Upper-East stamp, for example.

At his request, a girl drops off the card at the local mailbox. *When I'm back home,* Konrad thinks, *I'll have my mother get me all the stamps from Upper Silesia.*

Again and again, Napoleon makes sure that the fire is fed. The flames are reaching almost as high as some of the nearby houses now.

The first stars appear in the sky.

Still the people from Pietna remain with the soldiers.

Teuscher has brought out his accordion and plays all the songs of farewell and longing that he knows. And everyone else who knows how to play music takes out his instruments as well, whether it's an ocarina, a harmonica, or even just a pocket comb.

They sing songs like "Cologne, you beauteous Rhenish city" and "Whoever thought of separation."[74] Those simple songs, which will be continue to be sung for as long as men will go into battle.

Konrad has closed his eyes to fully take in this beautiful mood.

His heart opens wide: so this is the evening before battle! Singing, the soldiers consider the gravity of their decision. They do not speak a word of their sacrifice. Instead, they weave their longing for action into such inconspicuous songs!

Felix Teuscher begins a new tune.

First he plays soft, solemn chords. Then, gradually, the melody becomes audible.

Without any kind of command, the soldiers have gotten up from their seats. The men and boys of the village have removed their caps.

Verses resound into the deep twilight:

Morgenrot, Morgenrot,	*Sunrise, dear Sunrise,*
Leuchtest mir zum frühen Tod.	*Shine on my early demise.*
Bald wird die Trompete blasen,	*The trumpet soon will blow*
Dann muß ich mein Leben lassen,	*Then it's my time to go*
Ich und mancher Kamerad!	*With a comrade by my side!*

No one is much surprised that the women and girls in the audience have hidden their faces inside their aprons.

After the song, conversations falter. The men's thoughts circle over distant, uncertain things.

Napoleon stares into the dwindling fire and does not prevent it from burning out.

Suddenly, Lemke's command rings out in the silence.

The soldiers take up arms. In just a few minutes the Freikorps is ready to march.

The village women have hurried over with flowers and twigs.

Still holding their caps, village men and boys look after the soldiers until their columns have been absorbed by the darkness.

Maßmann has given orders to avoid any unnecessary noise, so the men march in silence.

---

[74] "*Köln am Rhein du schönes Städtchen*" and "*Wer das Scheiden hat erfunden*" were popular folk songs from the early twentieth and late nineteenth century, respectively. They deal with themes of love, separation, and nostalgia.

About half of a mile behind Pietna, a large number of carriages are waiting, discreetly commandeered at the last moment. The drivers have been told that they will be shot if they make even the slightest attempt to attract the enemy's attention. But almost all of them are good Germans at heart and wouldn't even think of treachery.

Horseshoes have been torn off. Cigarettes have long since been extinguished as well.

And so the columns drive through the night. Like a ghost, silent and eerie. It is rare to hear a rifle barrel clattering against a steel helmet, and even rarer to hear a horse stumble or neigh.

Not a single shot is fired by the enemy.

Without any incidents, the Freikorps is unloaded at the gates of Krappitz. The clock strikes midnight as the columns line up in the empty town square.

As if on command, the full moon emerges from its veil of clouds, casting its pale yellow light onto the steel of helmets and rifles.

Maßmann stands in a slightly raised position.

Planted right next to him, their flag rustles in the night wind.

The men stand in silent expectation, their rifles pressed tightly against their bodies.

Maßmann raises his head.

His voice is clear and hard. Not one of his words is lost to the audience.

"Comrades! We are about to face the storm. Two hours from now, we will have to prove that our German will to live is stronger than the fury of our enemies who have been allowed to triumph until today. In two hours hence, we will challenge fate and ask it whether Germany's honor shall rise or sink into eternal night. We are the first of our folk to have found our way back. A way that leads us to ourselves. Remember this when we plant our flag, the sign of our victory, at Annaberg. Remember this when the enemy iron tears us apart. Just as we intend to crown our bold deeds with victory, so too we want to be ready, if necessary, to lay down our lives for our idea—as a sacrifice to our struggle for freedom and as an example for those who will fight for freedom after us. I do not need to appeal to your courage. You came to arms out of your own free will, so you have already proven it. Now I appeal to your recklessness, your rebel spirit. That spirit with which you will lay down your lives for victory, even though prudent thinkers and know-it-alls may deem it impossible. Grow beyond the norms of bravery. Grow into those dizzying heights of loneliness and greatness. The greatest of the German nation! This is no longer an order! This is a message from a new world, that either begins with your victory, or, through our deaths, rises to the stars above, as a dream. A shared dream, desired not just by us, but generations to come!"

The Freikorps takes up starting positions.

Silently the men march into their positions and receive ammunition.

One first aid kit is distributed for every two men.

Like all the men in his assault squad, Konrad receives four hand grenades. He hooks them onto his belt, two on each side.

The full cartridge belt pulls down on his neck, forcing Konrad to jerk himself up again and again. The hand grenades pull down his belt and hit against his knees. He doesn't really know how long he will have to march like this. All he knows is that he's extremely tired and that the fog is soaking his uniform and paralyzing his joints. A few times he stumbles and would have fallen if not for his comrades grabbing and supporting him at the very last moment.

The starting position of the assault squad is a deep trench on the edge of a small village. One can barely see twenty to thirty yards ahead through the thick morning fog. The stars are fading, and the sky has taken on a cold, dark gray hue.

Konrad lies in the ditch and peers into the fog.

So this is where death is lurking? Over there, beyond this sparse rye field whose stalks are not yet a foot high?

Still no enemy movement. The silence weighs heavily on the men's feverish nerves.

If only the first shot would be fired already!

The silence is eerie.

Tonight, even the nearby village dogs are silent.

Chapter 27

On May 21st, at around 2:15 a.m., the final assault troop segments take up their positions, unnoticed by the enemy. Everything happens smoothly, all according to plan.

The line Krempna-Jeschona has been assigned to the right wing of the attack columns.

The Chappuis column is ready with its Freikorps!

Von Watzdorf's battalion is in reserve near Ottmuth, just as they have been ordered.

The attack column Horadam is faced with substantial technical difficulties in their march toward their starting positions.

With a dogged, furious determination, the Oberlanders have secured the most difficult part of the task for themselves.

Horadam is fully aware that his column will have to push into a formidable, yet narrow, ravine, whose slopes are equipped with all kinds of light and heavy armaments, both to the left and the right. He knows that any prolonged delays in the planned assault run will inevitably lead to a complete wipe of his corps. That is why he is delighted that von Eicken's brave men from the Gogolin battalion are leaving their defensive position, practically deserting toward the enemy. To the east of Gogolin, rifles in hand, lies the first battalion Oberland under Lulu Östereicher, who can barely contain his impatience. He has been given the task of charging against the Strebinow-Groß-Strehlitz line. He knows that this task is outrageously large, and difficult as well. A true daredevil, he is all the happier that it has been entrusted to him.

If only his people were a little better-armed, he thinks. Some of his companies are eerily reminiscent of hiking clubs. Instead of rifles, one can see a number of men clutching oaken walking sticks. A particularly sturdy Tyrolean wields a club of a girth which would befit a Heracles.

The second battalion Oberland, led by Captain Ritter von Finsterlin, is right behind the first battalion. It has received orders to form the second wave of attack after the advance of the Austrians.

On the north side of Gogolin, toward the Kalk mountains, lies the third Oberland battalion under Major Siebringhaus. They are accompanied by Storm Commando Heinz, waiting for their attack orders.

Areas to the south are held by the Black Band Freikorps, which is joined by the Black Guard.

At 2:29 a.m., Maßmann is standing in the trench next to the assault squad, luminous watch in hand.

Konrad can feel his heart beating, leaping against his chest.

His eyes are glued to the lieutenant's lips.

Five more seconds until the command!

Five more seconds until relief.

"Get up, march, march!"

Fifty throats join in an extremely croaky "hurrah," only to be drowned out the very next second by the excessive drumming of machine gun fire. The first great attack wave has begun.

For a moment the enemy seems speechless with surprise, but then the bursts of their heavy machine guns sweep across the flat field.

Martin Harke knows how to handle his assault squad. Like snakes, the men wind their way through the field, toward the next elevated patch.

As the fog gradually disperses a little, the muzzle flash of enemy machine guns become visible.

Harke notices that the enemy machine gun nests have been placed in a very efficient pattern throughout the small hills overlooking the field.

He scans the hills with his binoculars. Fifteen nests in total. He also manages to spot a system of trenches about fifty yards below the nests. *Damn it!* He thinks. *If only we had a single proper cannon!* In the meantime, Lemke has led his first company to the trench, ordering the men to fan out across the area.

Fuchsberger waves the flag. He runs across the field, erect, roaring his furious hurrah.

Maßmann hurries toward the second company to have Teuscher bypass the ridge.

Furious roars can be heard from the direction of Gogolin. Apparently the Oberland battalion is also encountering considerable resistance.

The enemy batteries are fully awake now.

The first shell hits just ten yards in front of the assault squad's slightly-elevated bump in the field. Konrad spits out mouthfuls of sand. A grenade splinter whizzes right past his steel helmet, missing it by a razor's edge. Instinctively he ducks his head deep into the stalks.

Harke has been watching him and laughs.

"Don't bother, Konrad. Once you hear them whistling and buzzing, it's already over. You just need to worry about the ones that you can't hear."

Konrad is ashamed. Silently, he has to admit that he is unbelievably scared.

It certainly wasn't like this around last night's campfire. Back then, everything still seemed so easy, like it was just natural to head out into the fire. And where were those good intentions now? What was left of his heroism? He sinks his teeth into his lips until he can feel a warm trickle running down his chin. *Let no one notice what a pathetic coward I have become*, he thinks. Then he notices a cold-blooded Harke carefully setting up a light machine gun.

With the machine gun in position, he starts to unload on the enemy.

Konrad sees a jet of fire streaming forth from the barrel, sweeping into an enemy machine gun nest.

Behind them, he can hear Lemke's voice. So the first company is already close.

The enemy's machine guns no longer fire as high as they did just a few minutes ago. They have zoomed in on their target. More and more frequently, the bullets start to slap into the sandy ground right in front of Konrad. He squeezes his eyes shut. What if they hit? Will it really just burn?

There, finally—Harke trills on his whistle.

What a relief! The advance continues.

The assault squad hasn't fired a shot yet. Harke wants them to hold their fire until the very last moment.

The men crawl forward as fast as they can.

Konrad barely notices the thistles scratching his face. All he can feel is his fear disappearing as he moves forward.

The first screams of wounded men hit his ears. The enemy bullets have begun to find their target. Suddenly he sees that comrades to his left and his right are rolling on the ground in agony.

Harke has ordered them not to waste any time on bandaging.

They leave that task to the paramedics, who follow behind the first wave of soldiers. The assault squad has to focus all its strength on the target.

Suddenly Konrad trembles. The man next to him has been shot through the chin. His head looks terrible, disfigured. And now the man turns to him and slurs something which he doesn't understand.

Another bump in the terrain. A moment's pause for breath.

They have come to within about a hundred yards of the enemy trenches.

Fortunately, enemy rifle-fire is still aiming too high. Poor first and second wave—they will have to deal with it.

One comrade cries out and thrusts up his hand. The palm is completely torn asunder. Harke turns pale with rage. "Those blokes over there are using explosive rounds."

Then he takes up the light machine gun and pelts the enemy with salvos until the barrel turns red with heat.

They receive their firing orders.

It only takes a first shot for Konrad to calm down remarkably. This is just like sniping in the camp. Slowly clean the barrel! Take time to aim! Carefully insert the framed cartridges!

He fires off twenty rounds. Those bright uniforms over there are easy to recognize against the ground. You can even make out their faces. The best thing to do is to aim at about two inches below the steel helmet!

The first enemies break away from the trench, trying to hurry away. Konrad can clearly hear the curses and commands of their officers. A flag becomes visible, its white eagle shining across the field. Harke pulls around his machine gun around and fires into the group. They collapse in mere seconds. The white eagle disappears under a pile of fallen men.

Thirty or forty men have begun to climb out of the trench, looking to throw themselves against the storming Freikorps.

Harke raises his hand. Ready the hand grenades!

Konrad twists the capsule off the shaft. The white ball falls out, hanging an inch below the shaft.

Harke blows on the whistle. The men leap up in unison and rush forward.

Konrad is surprised to see that it's no longer all fifty of them jumping up. They have lost men.

But he has no time to pursue that thought. In a small hollow nearby, there are five insurgents, rapidly firing at the men. In a flash, Konrad throws himself to the ground and crawls closer. He's carefully holding the hand grenade, to prevent the small white ball from accidentally hooking itself on a straw somewhere. He is only about eighteen or twenty yards away now, crouched down like a tiger. His tensed muscles are as hard as iron. He is dominated by a single thought, compelled by just one instinct: to throw the hand grenade right between the enemies. With a powerful jerk, he yanks off the ball. There's the hiss. Now the count. Calmly.

He counts down under his breath, just as he has been taught.

"Twenty-one, twenty-two, twenty-three!"

At twenty-three, he jumps up to a crouched position, throws the hand grenade toward the target, and presses himself to the ground again. The detonation roars over to him. He can hear screams. Lifting his head, he sees three insurgents rolling around, screaming, another one running up the hill as fast as he can manage, and a fifth laboring hard to drag himself after him.

As he readies the second hand grenade, Konrad no longer hears the thud of the shells. He is entirely absorbed by the frenzy of battle.

Almost as if in a fever, he runs toward the first trench, throws a grenade, presses himself to the ground, then throws another one. Jumping over the trenches, he can already see the first of his comrades near the machine gun nests. One after another is taken out by hand grenades. Enemies spared by the bullet are bludgeoned with rifle butts. Having thrown his last grenade, he pulls the rifle from his back. He shoots from ten, eight, then five yards away. Yellow uniforms cover the earth. Terrible screams tear through the air, drowning out the crackling of rifle shots and the crashing of grenades.

Then, suddenly, silence.

A silence that is strangely painful.

The first rays of the sun make their way across the battlefield.

Enemies flee in thick crowds.

Harke has planted one of the captured heavy machine guns and mows them down with grim determination.

Exhausted, the men of the assault squad stand about, breathing heavily. As they wipe the sweat from their faces, Konrad looks back.

There's the men of the first company. Several yards ahead of them, the lieutenant and Lemke. Behind them Fuchsberger with the flag. A few minutes later they have caught up to them. Maßmann beams at the assault squad. "Damn fine job, boys!"

Harke stops firing, stands up and walks heavily toward Maßmann. He is quite embarrassed when the lieutenant squeezes both of his hands.

Fuchsberger counts the bullet holes. Seven shots have pierced the flag, an eighth one has splintered the shaft.

Far behind them, the paramedics are going about their business. They hardly know where to start.

Maßmann turns to Lemke.

"It's almost a miracle that there are more yellow than gray uniforms lying about."

Harke waves them over. He has found an opened box of cartridges. Full of indignation, he points to a green ring marking the casings.

"There's our proof that they've been using explosive bullets."

Maßmann's face takes on a hard look.

"An eye for an eye!"

Each man of the assault squad grabs ten frames of the marked cartridges.

Shells whiz down in rapid bursts. The enemy, having realized that the ridge is lost, unloads all of their firepower on the area.

Harke blows the signal. "Assault squad, march!"

The weapons captured over the course of the battle are almost exclusively of German origin.

It is noticeable that Haller soldiers are deployed in large numbers around Annaberg. Regular soldiers. And when the enemy artillery fire turns particularly potent, every single volunteer in the German Freikorps knows that the enemy gunners are being directed by French citizens!

Chapter 28

The Germans are advancing victoriously all along the line.

After the initial surprise-attack, they have begun to face strong enemy resistance everywhere.

A highly effective barrage shows just how familiar the enemy has become with the area.

The battle has barely lasted three hours and the Freikorps leaders are relieved to see that their men have managed to supplement their missing armaments with enemy equipment.

The third Oberland battalion has joined forces with volunteers from Storm Commando Heinz. In a furious assault, they expel the insurgents from the Kalkberg area, previously considered impenetrable due to the enemy's superior position and armaments.

Pushed by initially heavy losses, rage turns to frenzy. As the clash comes to a close, hardly any shots are being fired. Rifle butts and knives make short work of the enemy.

Wherever the first Oberland battalion fights, enemy resistance is overrun.

The insurgents flee, leaving their strategic positions at Vorwerk Strebinow[75] to the Bavarians.

Bergerhoff's troops encounter heavy resistance and are stopped in front of the Wygoda Heights. The attackers have to endure dangerous fire against their flanks.

The road to Groß-Strehlitz is blocked by a heavy barrage. Transports

---

[75] A *Vorwerk* is a large agricultural estate, historically located outside fortifications such as castles or city walls.

of German wounded to Krappitz are ongoing. Driving out the enemy of the Groß-Steiner forest is not yet feasible, because there simply are not enough soldiers available to clean up the seemingly endless forest areas.

So without further ado, they disregard the forest and commit to a frontal attack, storming directly toward the enemy!

Storm Commando Heinz makes its way through the devastating barrage from within the forest to snatch the dominating Sakrau Hill from the enemy.

Together with the third Oberland battalion, they stop for a brief moment in order to catch their breath.

The fighting is becoming more and more bitter on both sides. They fight tooth and nail for every single machine gun nest, every single farmhouse. It is close combat until the very last man has been finished off.

The first Oberland battalion does not stay in Strebinow for long. Despite raging flanking fire from the Wygoda Heights, they storm the Neuhof *Vorwerk*, the Sakrau estate, and the Red Mountains.

By now the morning is well underway. The sun is burning down mercilessly from the sky.

The blood of the wounded is drying to thick crusts, and thirst has become almost more troublesome than the enemy iron. Men risk their lives to draw a drink from a well under open fire.

The few peasants and farm laborers that haven't long since fled the area are cowering in the cellars of their huts and houses, frightfully praying to their saints to save their lives.

Whenever a shell hits a roof, huge flares rise toward heaven. The inhabitants would rather get buried under smoking debris than risk an escape into the open, where bullets and grenades are threatening their lives.

High up on horseback, mounted messengers dash through the terrain. Motorcycles are mostly unusable, because the country roads have become impassable as a result of the continuing barrage.

Horadam curses. He has trouble keeping his nerve, seeing how Lulu Östereicher's first battalion is gradually being forced to abandon their straight assault by highly effective enemy fire from the Wygoda Heights. They already had to make some adjustments toward the south.

Again and again Östereicher raises his fist to the Wygoda Heights: a silent threat. He is not at all content to be pinned down by enemy fire. His men in particular deserve to pin the laurels of victory to their flags.

The second Oberland battalion still lies in reserve near the Gogolin road. Horadam decides to throw them into the battle.

A mounted messenger dares the foolhardy ride through a seemingly endless hail of bullets, delivering the order to Captain von Finsterlin. The men of the second battalion can hardly be contained. They are eager to enter the fray, complaining that the others must have forgotten them in this uninviting hamlet.

The second battalion consists for the most part of thick-headed Westphalians and taciturn North Germans who consider it a disgrace having to play backup for the advancing South Germans. A roar of joy rises as von Finsterlin orders them to march.

Their companies storm along on their death march to Groß-Strehlitz, unstoppable, despite a devastating barrage of enemy bullets.

With dogged defiance, the second battalion repeatedly launches their frontal assaults. In the end, their bloody sacrifices gain them a first victory.

Dombrowka has been taken!

The Westphalians are reassured: their northerner deeds are looking quite respectable next to those of their southern comrades.

At the foot of the Wygoda Heights, things are looking gruesome. Bergerhoff's Black Band is close to being routed. Again and again his brave troops charge across the brutally open terrain; again and again their waves are repelled by shot and steel.

The men's eyes tear up with anger. They know that victory itself depends on them taking this fortress of a hill. They know that without control over the Wygoda Heights, storming Annaberg is impossible.

They can feel that the other Freikorps leaders are with them in thought, that their comrades at Sakrau, Dombrowka, Neuhof, and Strebinow are watching them with longing, eagerly waiting to finally see the German flags wave from this mountain.

The Black Band's flag-bearer falls, pierced by five bullets. A young volunteer snatches up the sacred sign and carries it forward. He too dies a soldier's death after barely advancing another hundred yards.

Bergerhoff looks around, searching for anything that could help. No god can conjure up cannons or men for him. Yes, the Bavarians have captured two large field guns, but they urgently need them for their Lembert assault battery. And replacements? Any Freikorps would be glad to have those. The only ones who have yet to suffer significant losses are the Strachwitzers. But they are pinned down at the Groß-Steiner forest and can't seem to break away.

Lensch and Winkler's Freikorps are being bled dry in front of Oberwitz. Winkler's bicycle company is suffering particularly heavy losses. Those dashing lads are riding their bikes practically all the way into the enemy machine gun nests. Many of them get mowed down in the process.

The entire right wing of their assault is in jeopardy. Horadam has to endure a couple of nerve-wracking hours. There he sits, hunched over his map, waiting for news of the Chappuis column which could be routed at any moment.

The mounted messengers are delivering increasingly bleak news—if they return at all.

Chapter 29

Maßmann and his Black Guard are lying in a ditch, lining an avenue of cherry trees for almost half of a mile.

Concentrated enemy fire is hammering into the trees, which have long since given up their blossom branches under the hail of bullets. The German machine guns are still pounding every now and then. Rifle-fire has ceased because ammunition is about to run out. All but one frame of cartridges had to be delivered to the machine guns.

Konrad sits next to Heenemann and fits cartridges into the machine gun belts. They have to hurry, as the filled belts are virtually snatched away from under their hands. Maßmann leans against a tree, peering incessantly through the looking glass. The cigarette in the corner of his mouth has gone out. His face looks worried and tired. He has stopped sending out messengers because it just seemed pointless.

Grenades from the enemy batteries are hitting the avenue in intervals of one and two minutes. The men are pressed flat against the trench walls, happy if they manage to be spared by the splintering stone. They do not fear the iron, because the shell fragments just whiz right over their heads. And experience has it that direct hits rarely venture into a narrow trench.

Fuchsberger's flag is scorched, riddled with bullets. Now it lies at the bottom of the trench, neatly rolled up, and with a scorching heart Fuchsberger waits for the moment when he can finally unfurl it to storm anew.

A heavy machine gun has been finished off by a direct hit. Five men lie dead, gathered around the ruined weapon as if they were sleeping peacefully. An old cherry tree, cut down by many inches of shrapnel, has lowered itself over them, covering their blood with its blossoms.

Napoleon has been shot in the upper left arm. He refuses to leave his third company until finally Maßmann grows seriously angry and orders him to get bandaged at Krappitz. "You can give my warmest regards to my wife. But for heaven's sake, don't tell her how miserable the situation is around here!"

Grumbling, Napoleon trudges away. With a mix of anger and recklessness, he walks upright along the road. Konrad doesn't even dare to look after him, fearing that he will have to witness his death.

"No rest for the wicked!" Napoleon roars back at them before he disappears from the gaze of his comrades.

The men are gradually regaining their sense of humor. Heenemann in particular considers it his duty to set an example of superior courage for his younger comrades. With brash words and cocky talk, he waves a machine gun belt that has just been filled and climbs over the edge of the trench to deliver the ammunition to a rifle mounted five yards ahead in the open field. Once again he waves to his comrades. Then he suddenly grasps for his heart, stumbles around twice, and collapses in silence.

Konrad screams, rushes toward Heenemann, and drags him back into the trench. Relentless tears are streaming down his cheeks.

Then he crouches down next to the fallen man, not even noticing that he has laid him onto the rolled-up flag and that bright red blood is slowly seeping onto the cloth.

With a leap, Maßmann has reached Heenemann. He opens his tunic and pauses in shock as the blood-soaked image of little Ulrich falls toward him, pierced by a bullet hole.

Konrad has turned away and sobs, completely aghast. And many men who had grown fond of Heenemann are not ashamed to show their tears.

Harke takes over the leadership of third company.

The assault squad is distributed among the three companies for replenishment.

Chapter 30

At Oberglogau, all hell has broken loose.

The phones are buzzing incessantly. Suddenly the whole world wants to speak to the general. The chief of staff wrings his hands, gradually beginning to doubt the old man's sanity. He is more amiable than ever. Whether the callers are secretaries of state, the ministers themselves, or even the very office of the Reich president, he always gives them the same answer, with the same, unchanging smile.

Yes, it was true that the Freikorps had attacked. The battle was in progress and the outcome could not yet be foreseen. No, he could not order the corps to retreat, they had never been under his command, and besides, he had to refuse any measures that could confuse the troops at this very delicate moment!

The republic's foreign policy authorities have become hysterical. But this means war! Stop this at once! The general just smiles. His infinite regrets, but, alas!

Only when the Reichswehr liaison calls does he become serious. The situation was very precarious, with their losses exceeding even the worst of predictions. Simply a logical result of these insane border blockades![76]

At Breslau and Frankfurt, barracks have been locked down. The soldiers are on standby. Their officers are not sure what is going to happen over the next few hours.

The general instructs his chief of staff to answer telephone calls from

---

[76] The Weimar government actively hindered volunteers from travelling to Upper Silesia at the time of the Polish insurgent attacks. Aspiring Freikorps and self-defense battalion volunteers had to use deception and sometimes even force to make their way into the region.

Berlin on his behalf.

Less than half an hour later, the chief of staff is already using the same amiable, non-committal phrases, silently begging the general's forgiveness.

The general stands bent over the map. His hands tremble as he inserts the flags.

The mood at the insurgents' headquarters has hit rock bottom.

In Polish, French, and German, people are cursing, commanding, whispering, and shouting.

Reserves are brought in on trucks and directly thrown into battle to save whatever can still be saved.

The Wygoda Heights are their one, only, and greatest hope.

Therefore, more reserves to the Wygoda Heights!

Let it become a new Verdun!

Let the Germans bleed themselves dry on this hill!

The telephone lines to Warsaw are constantly occupied.

The German advance must not succeed!

To think that the Germans might actually take Annaberg!

At the Leschnitz station, the "Korfanty" armored train has been fired up, waiting for its movement orders and more than ready to hurl its devastating shells into the German ranks.

At the foot of Annaberg, insurgent battalions are preparing for their counterattack.

Catholic priests have blessed their flags. So far, the Virgin and all the other saints have been on the side of the insurrection! So go forth and advance against the accursed Germans!

New battalions hurry to join them from the Wyssoka Forest to deliver a fatal blow to the German corps. Guns and mortars, heavy machine guns and grenade launchers are brought in. The counterattack has to be deadly! With flags waving, the insurgent storm troopers attack. Their march is preceded by a murderous wall of shrapnel and grenades. Hissing infernally, the Korfanty train starts to move, crushing along the train tracks. Prayers can be heard: Almighty God, in the name of Christ and the Holiest Heavenly Virgin, grant victory to the white eagle!

A deluge of insurgents pours over the Ellguth Hills all the way toward Oberwitz. They are headed against the battered German front.

Von Eicken's men, the first and second Oberland battalions, Bergerhoff's storm troopers, and the Black Guard can hardly believe their eyes when they see concentrated enemy battalions approaching.

A cry of relief goes through the assault columns. At last, the enemy is coming in front of their muzzles!

They allow them to approach within a hundred, then fifty yards. Then, with a flash, they rain death and destruction into the enemy ranks. Dense rows of storming insurgents have turned into dense rows of corpses, with blood pooling around them.

Again the eagle flags are hoisted up, and again they sink to the bloodstained ground among the fallen flag bearers. No enemy is able to break through the German front, not even for a single step.

Horror seizes the insurgents. As their ranks are mistakenly hit by some of their own artillery shells, that horror turns into panic.

The survivors throw away their weapons and run for their lives. Only when they reach the railroad line do they stop and resume the defense.

One of the other men has been hit, so Konrad leaps toward the machine gun. Now his hands guide the cartridge belt. Burst after burst is fired into the enemy ranks. Heenemann has been avenged a hundred times over.

On the other side of the field, Bergerhoff's troops have already begun to storm.

Maßmann raises his arm. His three companies detach themselves from the trench and proceed to counterattack. Battle cries resound from all throats.

Konrad runs, his rifle cocked. Wherever an enemy jumps up in front of him trying to flee, he stops and aims, calmly and conscientiously as if this was just another day at the practice range.

With every shot he thinks of Heenemann. A hard gleam has entered his eyes.

There, five yards in front of him, lies an enemy. Konrad assumes him to be wounded and tries to run past. The insurgent slowly raises his rifle. For just a fraction of a second, Konrad stares into the small, eerily black hole of the barrel. Then he leaps forward and strikes with his rifle butt. A muffled crack and a vicious yelp penetrate his consciousness with an almost forceful clarity. He tastes blood. There is some kind of unknown matter sticking to his eyes. He slowly wipes his face with the back of his hand.

There's the man, lying in front of him, horribly disfigured. He has smashed his skull. Konrad stares down at himself. His uniform is covered with blood and splinters of skull. The butt of his rifle has been broken off.

He tastes a sickly sweet mass in his mouth and cannot help but to throw up.

Lensch and Winkler storm Oberwitz. Bergerhoff conquers the Wygoda Heights, supported by Maßmann.

Countless weapons are abandoned to the Freikorps.

The battlefield is littered with dead and wounded.

A few enemy assault battalions are still defending positions near Sakrau. They know that their return would endanger the Annaberg and proceed to fortify their positions.

Von Eicken's brave men advance close to their rear and entrench themselves at Vorwerk Dallnie in order to barrage them from this position.

Meanwhile, the second Oberland battalion is working its way across the heights, against Jeschona and Oleschka. Doggedly dragging themselves forward, the northern Germans are forced to watch the Bavarians of the first battalion reach Jeschona before them.

Horadam's worries are far from over. The concentrated enemy formations at the foot of Annaberg are giving him pause. It is simply impossible to push through this heavily-defended front. Also, the German battalions have been spread too far apart by their advance, losing some of their power.

Storm Commando Heinz has made the largest territory gains so far, overrunning Nieder-Ellguth together with the third Oberland battalion before entrenching themselves at Niewke. Already the first patrols are advancing against Kalinowitz, without a care in the world.

Horadam grits his teeth. On the map, it all looks picture-perfect. Annaberg appears to have been caught in their pincer. But they lack the men and material to close down on them!

If the insurgents were to use this moment to break away from Sakrau and drive their troops in a wedge toward Gogolin, the beautiful Freikorps pincer could be blown up right away. And then, forget about Annaberg!

Horadam is not exactly known for his nervous temper, but today, his nerves are stretched to the breaking point.

Speed is of the essence!

With every minute, they risk the insurgents realizing this fact, bringing about the final defeat of the storm! And then they can forget about the Freikorps spirit altogether. Then those clever tacticians and cool strategists would finally have their proof that it was all "impossible."

Horadam has decided to supply the official military staff with false reports about the current situation. If they had any idea what things were really like at the front, flags would already be flown at half-mast. Let them make up their own minds!

Should he halt the battle here and satisfy himself with what has already been achieved? So far, they have gained plenty of terrain. But who is to defend this front, now that it has suddenly ballooned to these enormous proportions? Who could build these positions into an effective defense?

No, only a total victory can save them. Any partial victory could bring about their complete defeat the very next day.

He wipes the sweat off his forehead.

What a damned situation!

Freikorps combat has always been a game of *vabanque*.[77] It's no use; they'll have to reshuffle the cards once more! Oleschka threatens to become another Wygoda. Just don't allow them to tie the Freikorps to a single place yet again. The troops can't survive a standstill, and neither will their assault strategy.

Hurry! Hurry! Hurry!

Horadam races his pencil across the notepad.

Horsemen race away into all directions.

Cyclists gasp, their craned necks hovering over the handlebars.

The first Oberland battalion is rapidly removed from the Oleschka death funnel.

Lulu Östereicher can give his men a brief respite. Parts of the second battalion remain in front of Oleschka, now tying down the enemy to this treacherous place.

Von Eicken too can withdraw his company from Oleschka.

A heavy load is taken off Horadam's mind when he receives the message that all the disengagements have been carried out, all according to orders. He can be sure that the North Germans of the second battalion led by von Finsterlin will not allow the enemy to leave. Thank God for those stubborn Westphalians! They will have their work cut out for them!

---

[77] "Vabanque" is a gambling term, originating from pharo, a French card game. The expression "*va banque*!" means that a player bets the equivalent of the money currently available to the game's banker—typically a very large amount, similar to an all-in situation in a poker game.

If only those constant inquiries from the command posts would stop bothering him so much. Horadam gives them nothing but lies, gaining time for carrying out his plans. He claims that things are looking bad. Next he reports the exact opposite.

"My men are about to storm! That's that!"

"Well, the front has become completely muddled, because the Freikorps are simply operating all on their own!"

To make matters worse, Horadam has just received word that Storm Commando Heinz and the third Oberland battalion, who launched that dashing assault on Niewke, have completely disregarded the Ellguth Hills. These have now been occupied by a group of enemy soldiers, allowing them to threaten the Germans from superior and secure positions.

All German assault squads are fully occupied. There are no reserves which could be employed to resolve this issue. Horadam and his staff officers decide on a daredevil approach.

Silent like cats, the officers stalk toward the enemy, before launching themselves at the soldiers. There is tremendous shouting, shooting, strangling, and stabbing, until at last the Germans are victorious. Their surprise attack was a complete success; no insurgent has been left alive.

A quick glance on the part of the officers reveals the tremendous impact of capturing the Ellguth Hills. The enemy immediately unleashes furious machine gun fire from the neighboring heights of the Wyssoka Forest. But the Germans have captured two guns near Sakrau, clearly of German origin. These guns are now being dragged into position by the officers: a laborious process. The gun-shields are completely dented, enemy machine guns are rattling against them like peas poured out into a box. Nevertheless, none of the daredevil officers are seriously wounded. It's a good thing they're not counting graze shots, or almost all of them would have to report back to the field hospital.

A very young lieutenant throws around the gun carriage. "Enemy battery! They're about to set up against us over there!"

With a few expert grips, they set the shell's fuse.

Boom! There goes the first shell. *Boom!* The second. *Boom!* The third.

A moment later, the second gun has been readied as well.

Boom! Bang!

The enemy battery abandons their idea of a duel with the German guns. They are gone in a flash, leaving behind their dead and wounded.

Since he's already started shooting, the young lieutenant starts to look for other targets. A few shells silence some of the particularly irksome machine gun nests. Next they focus on the enemy columns, still defending Oleschka in superior numbers. The second Oberland battalion is given some breathing space.

When the first shells hit the enemy ranks, von Finsterlin still thinks he must be dreaming. Then he assumes it to be a mistake of the insurgent batteries, erroneously firing upon their own comrades. Bit by bit, he finally realizes that those are German guns, reaping a rich harvest from the enemy lines. As he observes the hopeless confusion the shelling is causing among the enemies, he quickly comes up with a plan.

He grabs eight of his most daring men, tall, blond boys from Westphalia who would have flirted with the devil himself if necessary, plus all of the available messengers and cyclists who didn't have the time to look for a rifle. With this patchwork assault force, he bypasses Oleschka and enters the enemy's flank and rear, unnoticed by the insurgents. The battalion's companies are waiting in feverish suspense, until a small yellow flag waved by von Finsterlin signals the beginning of their surprise attack. They rise to commence their storm.

As the first enemy machine gun bursts come flying, von Finsterlin's assault troop launches itself into their positions with a deafening roar. The enemies are stunned, believing themselves to be faced with a much superior force. They rush away head-over-heels, abandoning a fully cooked lunch to the Germans.

Oleschka has been taken!

In a few minutes the companies have reached the town.

The joy is indescribable.

Only six casualties have been inflicted on the battalion throughout the attack: an attack that seemed completely hopeless just a few minutes ago.

Triumphantly, the northern Germans wave their Oberland flags toward the Ellguth Hills.

A tribute for a brave deed that spawned further deeds!

Half an hour later, their regrouping is complete.

The enemy has been driven out from the entire line.

Horadam's attack formation presents a unified front.

Chapter 31

The Krappitz military hospital is overflowing. Those who are only lightly wounded lie in the garden, under flowering bushes and trees, listening to the thunder of battle. The sparse reports that make it to the hospital contradict each other. Most of them aren't exactly favorable.

Those of the wounded who came in with their rifles refuse to give them up. Under no circumstance will they allow themselves to be taken prisoner.

The moans of the severely wounded and dying permeate the hospital's halls and corridors. They also make their way to the wounded in the garden. Whenever she gets a free minute, Louise hurries away from the operating table to see the members of the Black Guard. They describe every phase of the battle in minute detail, including every order, every single word uttered by her husband. The pride she feels at the men's effusive praise of Karl has almost eclipsed her fear for his life.

When Napoleon arrives, fun and cheeky as ever, she is startled at first. But right away she rejoices at the chance to speak to one of her husband's most trusted friends.

Napoleon is more than willing to accommodate, immediately launching into a verbose recounting of the corps' heroic deeds in general, and his own in particular. Although he would have done some things differently—Louise cannot help but smile—their achievements were quite remarkable so far.

He didn't forget to relay Maßmann's greeting either. His talk could have continued for hours if the doctor hadn't come by to interrupt him.

"Let's see your arm!"

Napoleon flips back the military tunic he has slung loosely across his shoulder.

The doctor looks worried.

"I hope the bone isn't injured. Quite a considerable loss of blood."

Lying on the operating table, Napoleon suddenly refuses to be chloroformed.

"Just give me some booze instead!"

The doctor laughs and has Louise fetch a bottle of Black Forest *Himbeergeist*[78] from his room. Napoleon takes a hearty swig before gritting his teeth. It hurts a lot as the doctor pulls out the bullet.

"You're a lucky one. A hundredth of an inch further and the bone would have shattered!"

Napoleon smiles wearily. Louise tenderly puts on the outer bandages.

By the time the next wounded man has been delivered to the operating table, Napoleon has disappeared. Shaking his head, the doctor notes that only the tattered tunic remains. Napoleon took the bullet with him. And the bottle of Black Forest *Himbeergeist* as well!

The enemy is blowing up bridges and overpasses all along his retreat. They are certainly not trying to save on dynamite. Some of the heavy cobblestones are catapulted more than a half-mile away.

Horadam smiles with satisfaction. An auspicious sign for the progress of their battle! His index finger runs across the map. Up here at the Ellguth Hills, the first Oberland battalion has taken up positions.

Östereicher rejoices like a boisterous boy. By now his men have gotten enough to eat, and someone even managed to find some beer. His last communications already contained some slight taunts as to when they would finally get to move on. Did Horadam want to risk his Bavarians running off to the front on their own?

The second Oberland battalion has already moved beyond Oleschka to their new starting positions.

Von Finsterlin is growing somewhat impatient; he fears that the enemy will re-establish themselves if they do not continue their attack immediately.

The third battalion under Siebringhaus is waiting for their assault orders between Ober-Ellguth and Niewke.

---

[78] *Himbeergeist* ("raspberry spirit") is a type of alcoholic beverage, obtained by infusing highly concentrated ethanol with fresh berries, which is subsequently diluted with purified water until the mixture reaches about forty percent alcohol content. The Black Forest region is a particularly popular one for this kind of beverage.

Storm Commando Heinz and von Eicken's company have taken up positions at the edge of Wyssoka Forest, waiting for the moment when they can commence their race onto Annaberg.

Step by step, the Chappuis column conquers more enemy terrain. The insurgent retreat has slowed down considerably.

Connections between the individual Freikorps are constantly breaking down as each detachment gets entangled in special missions to conquer particularly tricky defensive nests.

The remnants of the Winkler bicycle company are lured into a trap and almost completely wiped out.

Freikorps Lensch has trouble keeping up as well, as they are constantly held off by heavy enemy fire.

Bergerhoff has regrouped his heavily decimated Black Band right in the face of the enemy and their rapid fire, leading them into battle with undiminished fervor. Fighting shoulder-to-shoulder with the men of the Black Band are the volunteers of the Black Guard.

Hunger and fatigue have vanished ever since the battle resumed.

Martin Harke got hit near Borek. He was just about to comb the village edge with a light machine gun, getting his rifle into position without any issues.

He managed to fire off thirty rounds, and then the rifle stopped. Maßmann examined his wounds: five shots through the chest. The enemy machine gunner was aiming well!

Fuchsberger is filled with irrepressible rage. He needs to avenge his friend Harke.

Maßmann gives his permission for Konrad to carry the flag.

He clutches the shaft with both fists. His temples are pounding from exertion. The flag is heavy! Putting one step in front of another, he no longer hears the whistling and whirring of enemy bullets. He just looks straight ahead, carrying the flag forward.

Fuchsberger throws his hand grenades into every single house in Borek from which shots were fired. Using some French "egg" hand grenades captured in Wygoda, he kills the operators of two heavy machine guns. Surely the gunner who hit Martin Harke lies among the dead!

Maßmann's heart has become heavy. Heenemann dead, Harke dead, Napoleon wounded! Those were the dearest of his comrades!

Death has been reaping abundantly among the men of the Black Guard.

The flag is hardly recognizable. Large pieces have been shot out from the cloth. Konrad feels every bullet that hits it.

The Krempna forest is host to another series of fierce, close-combat firefights.

Enemy fighters have entrenched themselves behind trees and hedges, opening their destructive fire at close range.

There is ample opportunity for Fuchsberger to apply his hand grenades. He develops great skill in sneaking up on enemy nests as well. No grenade is thrown in vain.

Suddenly infernal hissing can be heard coming from the railroad line. The Korfanty train has finally departed from Leschnitz and is headed to them via Roswadze, eager to finally unload its ruinous cargo. Shock troops advance under its protection.

One of Bergerhoff's companies tries to tackle the monster, using nothing but their rifles, and is completely annihilated.

The armored train comes to a halt and begins to hurl death against the Germans from all of its various pipes and barrels. Pistols, infantry rifles, and even machine guns simply bounce off its heavy armor. All the men can do is try and use rapid fire to prevent the enemy shock troops from leaving the safe area behind the armored train. They no longer think of cover; one after another stands up to shoot at every head that dares to advance from behind the train.

Bergerhoff is raging with fury. The armored train has already stopped their advance for a dangerously long time and is preventing the Annaberg pincer from closing.

Then Fuchsberger jumps forward, swinging a number of grenades in his right hand. With huge leaps he runs toward the monster and hurls the load between the rails.

There is a terrible crash. Splinters whir through the air. Loud screams prove that not even the enemy shock troops have been spared. The men use this moment of confusion to jump onto the railroad track and fire on the enemy at close range.

The armored train gives off three shrill whistles and steams away as fast as it can toward Roswadze, abandoning the shock troops in a cowardly display. They are cut down to the last man.

Fuchsberger has sunk to the ground. A ricochet has torn his left thigh to the bone. The wound doesn't seem to be life threatening once the leg has been tied off, though.

Maßmann strokes his hands.

"Thank you, Fuchsberger!"

The patient opts to threaten after the train with his fist. "That's for Martin Harke!"

Chapter 32

After the Korfanty train has been driven away, the remnants of the Chappuis column continue their attack.

Horadam's group advances with flags flying, pushing back the enemy from village to village.

The menacing Wyssoka Forest looms ahead, with its hollow paths, trap-like ravines, and impenetrable undergrowth. Trying to smoke out the enemy with grenades seems pointless. The Germans have no choice but to thoroughly comb through the forest, even at the cost of great sacrifice.

The insurgents have lost much of their former confidence after the white eagle has been pushed back one mile after another. That is why they fail to take advantage of the forest as the Oberlanders would expect them to do. Instead, they allow themselves to indulge in superstition, thinking that the heavens will prevent the German heretics from capturing their holy mountain. They are so preoccupied by these convictions that they completely forget to continue their barrage and don't even try to ambush and massacre some of the German corps as they make their way through the forest.

Horadam has trouble finding his way. The few paths that exist are utterly confusing and twisted. Instinct is still the best guide. And so the first battalion, ordered to cross the forest, simply focuses on always keeping the hillcrest beneath their feet.

Horadam marches next to Lulu Östereicher now, an unlocked pistol in his fist. Behind them a few men are towing the two field guns that have been accompanying the battalion ever since they left the Ellguth Hills.

Östereicher doesn't mind his men shooting more often than absolutely necessary. All the better for them if the insurgents think that whole regiments are advancing against them, rather than just four weak and very exhausted companies. The men are having quite a bit of fun hurling hand grenades into some of the ravines. The noise is incredible. It probably sounds like large-caliber mortars to the enemy.

The machine gun nests falling into the hands of the Bavarians have long since been abandoned. Unfortunately, the weapons were destroyed beforehand. Only the ammunition is still usable.

The noise of battle from Wyssoka is coming closer and closer. The third battalion fights its way forward, not even thinking about taking their requisitioned farmer's carriage, which mainly contains the heavy machine guns and captured ammunition cases, out of the fire zone. Fortunately, the two draft horses aren't sensitive. They pull ahead at a steady pace, just as if they were hauling grain or potatoes.

Von Eicken's company supports the third battalion.

They advance in great leaps and bounds.

Enemy resistance, still quite considerable just before Niederhof, is broken in close combat.

The Wyssoka castle courtyard is smoked out with hand grenades.

Von Eicken's men also storm Windmühlenberg, located between Wyssoka and Waldhof.

In front of the forest, the stormers are reunited, greeting each other with cheerful shouts. There they stand in the vale, the men of Oberland, von Eicken and Storm Commando Heinz, all of them looking up. Above their heads rises the towering wall of the Annaberg monastery: an impressive, almost menacing sight.

The tower of the monastery church extends into the sky like an extended fist.

Already the bursts of enemy machine guns can be heard again.

Horadam's commanding voice drowns out the noise.

The men unload their two guns, pointing their barrels toward the monastery.

Very close to their rear—somewhere near Waldhof—enemy fire is suddenly picking up again.

Scattered insurgent detachments have come to their senses and are mounting a desperate defense.

Once again the storm troops have to take up positions.

The enemy makes a furious advance from Leschnitz, summoning up their last strength.

The noise of battle swells once again.

The Korfanty train too has regained its courage, attacking the area between Zyrowa and Roswadze from its railroad tracks.

In front of the Roswadze sugar factory lie the exhausted assault companies of Bergerhoff and Maßmann.

The enemy has taken up positions in the broad factory halls and is combing the field with his machine guns. The other end of the field is occupied by the dwindling assault force. They try to wrestle down the highly effective insurgent fire, but all their attempts are in vain.

Maßmann realizes that two of his machine guns have become useless. The remaining few guns have become unsteady in their fire because the barrels are too hot. Jams are a frequent occurrence. Rifle fire isn't doing much either.

The enemy has started to pelt them with shrapnel. They know how to arrange their volleys so that they explode right above the German heads. Lifting your helmet above the edge of the low trench is highly inadvisable.

One of those volleys makes Maßmann laugh. A dud burrows itself into the sand, just a few yards in front of their position, and already Konrad has jumped up to get the thing. The old hound.

"Whoa, Konrad, have you gone mad?"

"I just thought I'd take the dud home with me, as a souvenir!"

Maßmann shakes his head in amusement.

"And what if that thing explodes once you try to pick it up?"

Ashamed, Konrad jumps back into the trench. He hadn't thought of that.

A cloud of dust approaches on the country road from Krempna.

Maßmann raises his binoculars. He still can't make out much. It looks kind of like a carriage.

The dust has caught the attention of the other Black Guardsmen.

"I see a horse!"

"Yep! You can clearly hear the horseshoes clattering!"

Maßmann lowers his glass in amazement.

"That guy must have more than a screw loose!"

Right. Now, unconcerned about the bullets and shells, a carriage is approaching over the uncovered country road. The nag looks ancient, moving at a tired, loping trot.

All of a sudden, Maßmann jumps up and runs toward the carriage.

"Napoleon!"

Yes, it really is Napoleon.

Bare-chested, he squats on a cart, one of his arms in a sling tied across his neck.

And the cart turns out to be a light mortar!

"Napoleon!"

His eyes are gleaming with mischief. He doesn't look left or right, seemingly ignoring Maßmann and the rest of his Black Guard comrades. With a jerk he drives through the narrow ditch, stopping twenty yards in front of it in an open field. A few seconds later, the horse collapses, riddled with countless bullets. Napoleon cuts the horse loose and straightens out the mortar.

Wheeeeeeeeeee!

The factory chimney collapses onto a heavy enemy machine gun firing behind it. Human bodies are whirled through the air.

Maßmann has caught up to Napoleon.

The two men exchange a deep look. Then they quickly get back to work. Fifteen of the dangerous canisters are hauled at the enemy until their machine guns fall silent.

Then Napoleon makes his report.

"Reporting in with light mortar, acquired at Krappitz. The wife is doing excellent. So am I!"

Maßmann swallows, unable to speak.

Then Napoleon takes up position in front of his comrades, waving a bottle.

"GFDC will set you free!"

The medicinal Black Forest *Himbeergeist* is shared equally among the men.

Roswadze is taken. In the factory the men fill their pockets with sugar, still chewing on it as they are back under heavy fire in front of Deschowitz and Solownia.

Bergerhoff leads the remnants of his Black Band with undying determination. Their fight lasts for hours, taking them beyond the Leschnitz station to the back of the town, where they secure an important road leading from Slawentzitz to Annaberg via Salesche and Lichinia. Now the enemy can no longer use this road for their escape. They lose countless soldiers as they try to flee from Annaberg, running straight into the fire of Bergerhoff's machine guns.

Horadam's artillery guns perform miracles.

It takes only a few well-aimed shells to quiet things around Annaberg. The posts built into the slope leave their machine gun nests and retreat without firing any more shots.

The resistance seems to be gathering strength around Poremba, but

Horadam does not wait for the enemy troops to arrive. After a short breather, his men rise and advance with wild cheers to take care of this final task.

In wild leaps the third Oberland battalion charges up the Wyssoka road.

Von Eicken's men and Storm Commando Heinz turn the joint storm into a race for the laurel wreath.

The machine gun squad of the Third Oberland battalion, first company, is the first to push beyond the marketplace of Annaberg. The monks can't quite believe that the white eagle has flown away. Silently, they begin to doubt the justice of their god, who decided to let the "heretics" have their victory.

Now the first Oberland battalion follows in broad waves. Ten yards ahead of his men rushes Lulu Östereicher, who is not at all amused that Siebringhaus and his third battalion have beaten him to the goal. Indignantly, he threatens with his fist.

Panting next to the third battalion runs the second, which has just smashed the last pockets of enemy resistance near Zyrowa.

Twelve tolls by the monastery bells.

The first German Freikorps soldiers start to mount their machine guns to intercept any enemy counterattacks.

Heavy guns rumble across the market square to keep Poremba and Leschnitz at bay.

Chapter 33

Maßmann and his Black Guard are fighting near Vorwerk Karlshof.

The sound of exploding hand grenades can be heard coming from the Leschnitz train station.

So Bergerhoff is already in close combat.

Napoleon has to conserve his mortar cartridges.

Heavy fire is coming from Kuhtal. Overwhelming the enemy is tough, because they are extremely well entrenched.

Slowly the men advance, in small storm waves, yard by yard. The fields offer hardly any protection against the enemy barrage. They lose more and more men, dead and wounded alike.

Finally, an assault by the second Oberland battalion creates some breathing space.

The enemy's fire becomes unsteady and falters.

Maßmann waves to his men.

Konrad waves their bullet-ridden flag high above his head, and the Black Guard advances in a broad line. They have to prevent the enemy from regrouping, pushing them away from the Kuhtal-Stockau road and out into the open.

Suddenly there's a machine gun at the Chapel of the Three Brothers. Before Napoleon can yank around his mortar to silence it, the first burst cuts into the German ranks.

Maßmann wipes his cheek. A graze shot has torn open his right ear.

Suddenly, a scream. Konrad is rolling on the ground, moaning. His hands are pressed tight to his body. An incessant stream of bright red blood seeps through his fingers.

Napoleon throws the first cartridge and shreds the machine gun nest with a direct hit.

No more shots are fired from the enemy side.

Maßmann has bent over Konrad, gently pulling his hands away. A ricochet has torn open the boy's body. There he lies, his eyes closed. All the blood has drained from his cheeks; his pale lips twitch in pain. Gently, the comrades lay him on a stretcher made from their rifles.

Slowly they carry him up the Annaberg. Foam has risen to his mouth, his eyes gleam dully. Maßmann holds his hand and tries to say something. In vain.

Cautiously, the porters take step after step.

One after another, the comrades push past them, wanting to see the boy one final time. Maßmann gives a sign to stop. Tenderly, he straightens out Konrad's head and points toward the Annaberg. That very moment, the German flag is hoisted up the monastery steeple, shining and fluttering in the wind. They can hear the German anthem being sung.

The men of the Black Guard take off their steel helmets and join in the song. And before they can even re-adjust their storm straps, Konrad's young life has come to a close with a final, ragged breath.

Maßmann takes up the tattered flag and holds it over the dead Konrad Ertel.

"I lived through Langemarck and Verdun. Those were the highlights of the Great War. Yet Annaberg shall be the symbol of a German youth, headed for a new world, to find their freedom!"

As the Black Guard occupies the road to Leschnitz, they encounter the First Oberland Battalion, clearing the slopes of a few scattered enemies.

Östereicher steps up to Maßmann and salutes.

"We have the Annaberg. But Germany is not yet free. Our fight continues!"

Horadam delivers his first truthful report to Oberglogau:

"After a series of bloody battles and heavy losses, German Freikorps stormed Annaberg on May 21st. The enemy's front was overrun, nine miles deep and sixteen miles wide.

"Six guns, countless machine guns, and other war material have been captured.

"The German Freikorps continue their victorious advance."

The general at Oberglogau advances his flags. His face beams with a happy smile, and his chief of staff gets to hear many profound thoughts about the faithful German youth.

Telephone calls from Berlin have become less frequent. The people over there seem to have resigned themselves to the changed circumstances. Perhaps they are also hoping that most of the rebels will never see their homeland again.

Far away from fearful cowards and hateful villains, the German Freikorps are marching toward the East.

Their flags bear one word: freedom. Their hearts beat to the rhythm of duty.

More than five hundred of them lie fallen along the roads and villages, the mountains and valleys they stormed. And the blood of those five hundred is calling out to them. It is calling so vehemently and compellingly that not a single one of them will ever find rest again, not until their flags are waving from the mountain of freedom, announcing the dawn of a new world.

Until that day, they are rebels. But on that day, they shall be the first citizens of a mighty empire.

The Aftermath:
A Military and Political Appendix

May 22nd

With very few exceptions, the German Freikorps continued to occupy the positions that had been conquered the previous day.

Freikorps Lensch and Winkler relinquish their hold of the conquered Wielmirzowitz-Kowalliksruh line due to tactical reasons and draw their troops closer to Leschnitz.

The Graf Strachwitz detachment breaks formation for further combat.

Bergerhoff and his Black Band drive back enemy raiding units operating out of Lichinia, advancing through Lichinia toward Salesche. However, he is forced to backtrack his troops at night, retreating toward Leschnitz.

A large enemy counter-offensive is expected, but never materializes. Instead, a number of small-scale battles break out, because German corps do not have sufficient manpower to form a closed-off front.

Messages of enemy troop movements are so severe that significant parts of the German units are forced to regroup.

The entire first Oberland battalion is assigned to Lulu Östereicher and kept in reserve at Annaberg.

Freikorps Winkler is relieved by the von Watzdorf battalion and joins the reserve at Roswadze.

German Freikorps are informed about large reinforcements to the enemy troops.

It is said that two battalions with almost twenty machine guns stand ready at Olschowa, with the same number of battalions and plenty of equipment distributed between Klutschau and Poppitz.

Salesche is said to be surrounded by a regiment. Lichinia has been occupied by another battalion.

May 23rd

The enemy counterattack is being executed with exceptional force. Heavy artillery fire against the German front lines is causing substantial losses amidst the Freikorps troops.

Bergerhoff and his Black Band are facing the brunt of the assault. At the Lenkau-Lichinia-Scharnosin frontier, the enemy is rushing against the thin German lines. At the same time they are throwing well-equipped storm troops against Groß-Stein.

The enemy counterattack starts out very promising. Particularly the Black Band is at risk of being completely wiped out.

At the last possible moment, Lulu Östereicher and the first Oberland battalion charge down the Annaberg, attacking the enemy's rear and flanks. The enemy is forced to retreat, taking heavy losses.

Dogged fighting for Leschnitz.

Oberland fighter Lieutenant Diebitsch manages to connect Bergerhoff and Oberland, despite having received a light gut shot two days earlier. He had to free himself from the hospital by force.

Oberland's intervention prevents the complete loss of the Black Band.

All available troops engage in a counterattack. The enemy is repelled at Leschnitz and forced to cede Lichinia, Salesche, Vorwerk Oberhof and Klutschau to the Germans.

Lulu Östereicher and his men are the main force behind this victory.

Von Finsterlin and his North Germans are equally forceful. His second battalion surprises the enemy at Scharnosin, expels them from Scharnosin Forest and drives them back toward Olschowa, through Vorwerk Johannishof.

At Olschowa, the German advance is completely halted by heavy enemy fire.

The third company is wiped out completely.

Von Finsterlin personally gathers a makeshift troop and attacks the enemy's rear.

Olschowa is finally conquered.

The Freikorps troops hold the new frontier spanning from Dollna over Olschow toward Salesche.

May 24th

To the great dismay of the Freikorps troops and their leaders, new orders are delivered from Oberglogau: they are to relinquish all areas beyond Leschnitz.

Allegedly the Inter-Allied Commission has agreed to authorize a plan for the complete demilitarization of the battlegrounds.

As the Freikorps leaders do not have the chance to come to a joint decision, some of them comply with the orders. Utterly infuriated, the remaining leaders have no choice but to follow them.

And so the demilitarization succeeds. The Freikorps stand at the ready, demanding a continuation of combat operations to vanquish the enemy once and for all.

May 29th

Oberglogau announces new orders, explicitly forbidding any offensive Freikorps maneuvers!

May 31st

Oberglogau follows up its orders with a direct appeal to the troops. This appeal contains a warning against any independent military adventures.

The German Freikorps desert toward the enemy lines!

At the behest of the Oberland, the German Freikorps assault the enemy who was just about to launch their own attack.

Once again there are tremendous losses, an unheard-of number of officers among them. The third battalion Oberland loses all of its officers.

Storm Commando Heinz succeeds in a number of exceptional challenges.

Rosniontau is taken.

Kalinow falls to them after heavy fighting.

The train tracks around the Schimischow station are blown up, completely preventing the enemy from deploying their armored trains.

Amidst the fallen enemies, there is also a number of French soldiers.

For strategic reasons, parts of the conquered territories have to be relinquished once again.

The Dollna front is now well-secured.

Fifteen machine guns have been taken.

Most importantly, the Oberland fighters have to be credited with the complete disruption of enemy reserves, an advantage that should not be underestimated.

Together with Diebitsch, Lulu Östereicher advances and takes Lichinia, defended by a full enemy regiment. The German side consists of barely two hundred men.

The Freikorps leaders decide to put all of their force into a third all-out attack on the enemy, with the goal of running them over and freeing the industrial settlements behind enemy lines.

The general in Oberglogau is completely opposed to this plan.

June 3rd

The enemy advances in an attack on all fronts once again, but is pushed back everywhere.

The German Freikorps urge rapid action, putting them into direct opposition to Oberglogau.

There are clear signs that an attack on the industrial installations at the Kosel-Gleiwitz-Hindenburg line would not just be of tremendous military value, but also provide the basis for large-scale resistance by the German population, led by the Freikorps.

Oberland acquires the necessary trucks to dispatch volunteers from the front and rapidly deploy them to the industrial area.

Oberglogau orders the trucks to be seized!

June 4th

German Freikorps attack key enemy positions around the industrial area, advancing along the Slawentzitz-Kuschnitzka-Klodnitz line.

Heavy fighting breaks out at Poppitz and Salesche, causing heavy losses.

The enemy uses a halt in the German advance to blow up the bridge across the Klodnitz River at Slawentzitz. After their conquest of Slawentzitz, the Freikorps realize that a French battalion has readied itself at Ujest to support the already vastly numerically superior enemy.

The attack on the industrial area has to be postponed. Without tractor trailers, an operation twenty miles behind enemy lines simply isn't possible.

The Freikorps have to reorder their battle plans; their hearts full of rage at Oberglogau and his officers who mistrust them, they attack the broad enemy front. They open a breach along the Klodnitz, from Kandrzin (or Heydrebreck) to Kosel-Oderhafen.

In a counter attack, four thousand enemy soldiers try to regain the strategically important bridges, supported by artillery and an armored train.

Enemy attacks are repelled at heavy losses.

June 5th

The German Freikorps defend their conquered positions and even manage to expand them, despite stubborn enemy attacks.

Despite close and bloody combat, they have taken over six hundred enemies.

June 10th

The enemy command has to admit that a total of eight thousand men have deserted their weapons.

The German government feverishly tries to think of ways to rid itself of the "Freikorps danger"!

Mid-June

The German government completely cuts off the Freikorps and leaves them to their fate.

French troops are thrown in front of the battered enemy front.

The German Freikorps have been completely and utterly betrayed!

October 20th

After a series of dishonorable clashes, the League of Nations ignores the pitiful German government and decides in favor of its foe, already beaten by the Freikorps.

The German rebels' sacrifice was robbed of its practical success. Yet their moral and spiritual victory was all the greater because of it.

Ingram Content Group UK Ltd.
Milton Keynes UK
UKHW011817090423
419869UK00001B/35